But now, as Alessandro stood on this narrow street, under the tempestuous Stockholm sky, the evidence was irrefutable.

Ann-Sophie was standing in front of him with a rolling suitcase in tow, and the word *round* didn't begin to capture her belly. *Lush. Ripe.* Those words continued to echo inside him, over and over, despite the fact that here on the street, he could only see a hint of this new development under her outer layers. Seven months of repressing her voice, her laugh, the way her body seemed to be made especially for him—everything came back so viscerally. The hints of new curves under her shawl made his hands clench with the need to touch her in all the ways he shouldn't. Because the hunger that gnawed inside him was mixed with the jumble of emotions he had spent his adulthood shutting off. He knew too well the kind of destruction these intense emotions brought from him.

He glared at her belly incredulously, focusing on the fact that she hadn't said a word about this situation to him.

"You are pregnant."

A sizzling new duet from Harlequin Presents debut author Rebecca Hunter!

The Carandini Legacy

Double the brothers...means twice the trouble!

Italian tycoons Massimo and Alessandro have climbed the downward spiral of their scandalous parents' empire. It took blood, sweat and tears to redeem the Carandini name. Finally, the twin brothers have the world in their hands. But now comes their biggest challenge yet, and there's a lot more than just their empire at stake...

Massimo Carandini is cool, calm and collected. His carefully selected fiancée, Catarina d'Avalos, will consolidate the stability of his business. But when Catarina refuses to be neatly filed away in her own marriage and flees, Massimo must track her down and convince her to return as his bride!

Read Massimo and Catarina's story in *Convenient Wife Conditions*

Nothing can disarm Alessandro Carandini and his notorious charisma. Yet he can't forget Ann-Sophie Svensson and the nights they shared seven months ago. Sultry memories have real-life consequences though—Ann-Sophie's pregnant! And Alessandro *will* claim her hand in marriage, no matter what it takes...

Read Alessandro and Ann-Sophie's story in *Heir to Italian Altar*

Both available now!

HEIR TO ITALIAN ALTAR

REBECCA HUNTER

MIX
Paper | Supporting responsible forestry
FSC® C021394

Recycling programs for this product may not exist in your area.

ISBN-13: 978-1-335-21378-5

Heir to Italian Altar

For questions and comments about the quality of this book, please contact us at CustomerService@Harlequin.com.

Harlequin Enterprises ULC
22 Adelaide St. West, 41st Floor
Toronto, Ontario M5H 4E3, Canada
www.Harlequin.com

HarperCollins Publishers
Macken House, 39/40 Mayor Street Upper,
Dublin 1, D01 C9W8, Ireland
www.HarperCollins.com

Printed in Lithuania

Rebecca Hunter is an award-winning author, reader, traveler, occasional college professor, full-time chocolate lover, and keeper of a very messy desk. Her books have won the National Excellence in Romance Fiction Award (NERFA), the HOLT Medallion and the VIVIAN Award. She writes witty, passionate stories about complex characters and intriguing destinations for Harlequin's Presents line. For reading and writing updates, photos and travel plans, join her newsletter on her website: rebeccahunterwriter.com.

Books by Rebecca Hunter

Harlequin Presents

The Carandini Legacy

Convenient Wife Conditions

Visit the Author Profile page at Harlequin.com.

To the fantastic Jerry Thompson,
for making a home for romance books
and our romance community at Books Inc.

CHAPTER ONE

"HE JUST WALKED IN."

"Is he with the countess?"

The whispers swirled around Ann-Sophie Svensson, and she turned, despite her best intentions. From across the crowded ballroom, Alessandro Carandini shone like a god, even among princes, CEOs and others who likely thought of themselves in such terms. Tall and built, he should have looked just like his twin brother, Massimo, and yet, to Ann-Sophie, he was so very different. His silky black hair curled up at the ends in a hint of unruliness, quite the opposite of Massimo's close-cropped cut, and his bronze skin gleamed a little brighter in the glittering lights of the chandeliers. The cut of his crisp, white shirt hinted at the taut muscles underneath, and his tailored trousers tapered at the waist. Wearing his suit coat at meeting after meeting, he had looked every bit the bold, smooth-talking businessman he was. Now, without it, rumors of the trail of heartbreak he left seemed grossly underestimated. Alessandro towered over the woman he was escorting into the room, a lovely brunette whose hair was held back with jewel-studded clips that sparkled in the lights. Definitely real diamonds, Ann-Sophie thought as she watched them from her corner of the room.

She tucked a stray strand of hair behind one ear, trying not to compare herself. She was of hardy Nordic commoner stock, raised by a single mother in a comfortable apartment at the end of the subway line south of Stockholm. Though her blond hair and blue eyes held some cachet in the world, she was more pretty-adjacent than pretty, let alone beautiful. Usually, Ann-Sophie was grateful for that. Being a beautiful woman had its downside when said woman wanted, for example, to be acknowledged for her skills. Or travel seamlessly through the world. But today, as she watched the bejeweled woman who was doubtlessly minor royalty place a graceful and strategic hand on Alessandro's arm, then look up at him and laugh, Ann-Sophie wanted to be a little less…well, regular.

Alessandro Carandini was the opposite of regular. He was excess incarnate. A glow seemed to emanate from him that went beyond his astonishing good looks. He had a charisma, a magnetism that animated everything around him.

"You're staring." Ann-Sophie's fellow interpreter, Monique, gave her a gentle tug at the elbow. "Not that I blame you."

Ann-Sophie flashed her friend an innocent smile. "Nothing wrong with dreaming."

Still, Monique gave her a skeptical glance. Swedish Connection Interpreting Services often paired Monique and Ann-Sophie for larger diplomatic events like these, as Ann-Sophie's specialties in Italian, French and

Spanish complemented Monique's expertise in a few Slavic and Germanic languages. They had both been with the agency long enough to have earned the trust of their most prestigious clients.

"I thought you had no desire to live in this world," said Monique, gesturing across the dazzlingly ornate ballroom, lit by the glow of countless candles. Ann-Sophie squirmed under her friend's scrutiny, reminding herself that Monique could not see the exquisitely intimate scenes that played through Ann-Sophie's mind. Her friend would never suspect that these longing looks came from a source much deeper than fleeting fantasies. But whatever the theories that played through Monique's mind, her friend did not voice them.

"I don't. I have enough." *Enough.* It was the word her mother had used so many years ago, a word that had put her life into an entirely new light.

"You do have enough," Monique agreed. "But a bit of excess could be fun, too, especially in the form of Alessandro Carandini. Despite his…"

Her friend did not need to complete this sentence. Ann-Sophie was very well acquainted with this man's reputation for a particular kind of excess.

"Excess is overrated," she said. "The newspapers are filled with stories of miserable, wealthy people behaving badly."

Ann-Sophie had always shied away from anything indulgent. She came from a country that valued *lagom*, a Swedish word that lacked a good translation, particularly here, in the glitter of the Côte d'Azur. *Just right* was the best equivalent, "like in the Goldilocks story," she told English speakers. At a young age, before she had understood just how much her mother had given up for her unexpected baby, Ann-Sophie had leaned in the direction of indulgence. She had embarrassing memories of demanding toys, visits to Gröna Lund for a day of roller coasters and candy, more toys and, finally, the ultimate request: a visit with her elusive father.

"I *need* to meet him," she had insisted.

"You will not meet your father," her mother had said, so gently that Ann-Sophie at last heard the finality in her voice. "You must learn to tell the difference between wants and needs, *älskling*. You have enough."

Something had shifted inside her after that conversation. Somehow, those words had done what years of refusals had not. Ann-Sophie finally understood that no amount of wanting would make their father appear. In the space of this devastating realization, she had seen how her want had become a trap, a never-ending thirst. Because she had allowed it to be.

Alessandro Carandini was currently a thirst-inducing want, ill-advised, and yet, she still found herself gazing longingly after the man tabloids called Italy's hottest playboy.

"You don't have to worry. He seems very taken by the countess he's talking to," Ann-Sophie said breezily, as if the sting of watching Alessandro with a woman of his own social class was just a fact of life.

Monique laughed. "I'm not actually worried."

Ann-Sophie laughed, too, and pretended it wasn't another twist of a knife in her gut. A knife that she herself had placed there.

Every attendee, from prime ministers to princesses, administrative assistants to interpreters, had been invited to this last night of celebrations. Those attending the weeklong negotiations between the biggest powers in Europe were government leaders, ambassadors, large international businesses and NGOs. She spent the days side by side with Swedish diplomats and business representatives, clarifying trade strategies that would bring the maximum benefits to all countries involved.

Ostensibly, tonight was different. She, Monique and the other interpreters were like any other guests, free to drink champagne and eat fois gras canapés alongside the royals and company presidents they worked for. However, even at these after-hours parties the interpreters tended to keep to themselves, enjoying a few sips of France's signature beverages from the edges of the ballroom. Ann-Sophie always felt a bit like she was looking in on a world she regularly visited but never truly belonged. And she was fine with this. She didn't have to feel at home here, even if it was technically her workplace, because there were so many other reasons she liked her job.

Even if she did feel more at home here in this ballroom, it would be her job to suppress anything that might make her stand out. Interpreters were supposed to fade into the background, not attract attention. This was yet another reason she hadn't said a word to Monique about Alessandro, not even yesterday morning as the two women wandered down the streets of Nice, with its brightly painted buildings and carefully laid stone streets. They had walked until they'd arrived at the cerulean blue of the Mediterranean, dotted with yachts and jutting white rocks.

"I've barely seen you this week," Monique had commented offhandedly. "Are you having a secret liaison?"

Her friend had laughed away her own comment and didn't seem to notice the heat that had likely turned Ann-Sophie's cheeks pink. They both knew how out of character a secret liaison would be.

But tonight, in this ballroom with its gilded sconces and exquisitely restored frescos, she was doing a terrible job at deflection. Tonight, her own feelings were on display for Monique and, likely, this entire ballroom of kings and princes and prime ministers. She couldn't take her eyes off Alessandro Carandini, even as she was well aware that it was both uncomfortable and unwise to reveal the ache of want that flowed through her. Want, not need, she reminded herself. The wisest course of action would be to leave, but her feet seemed to be anchored to the floor. Because tonight was the last night. When she got on the plane tomorrow, she would likely never see him again.

So Ann-Sophie turned away from Alessandro to the huddle of interpreters that had gathered in this corner of the room. She flashed Monique a smile and focused on the conversation as it wandered from local restaurant recommendations to beaches. When the string ensemble began to play, she forced herself not to look at the dance floor. The last thing that she wanted to see was Alessandro Carandini gracefully dancing—because, of course, he had mastered dancing the way he had mastered everything else—with another woman in his arms. Ann-Sophie smiled and laughed like everyone else, and as the conversation drifted from one language to another, she pretended that this ache inside her didn't matter. When a colleague asked her to dance, she turned him down, telling him—and herself—that she was both ungraceful and not in the mood.

But as her thoughts drifted, she had clearly tuned out the people around her because, suddenly, she became aware that no one was speaking. Instead, everyone was looking just over her left shoulder. Startled out of her thoughts, she turned and immediately saw what had caught the groups' attention. Alessandro Carandini was walking toward their corner of the room, and he was looking straight at her, as if he had been searching for her all night. Ann-Sophie's body stilled as her heart took off in her chest. She swallowed, trying to break the spell, telling herself it was just a glance as he made his way around the room, entertaining dignitaries. Even though she could have sworn there was a flash of something more complicated in it. Even though he wasn't looking away.

The closer he came, the more hope bubbled inside her, despite her best efforts to quash it. Alessandro did not seem to be headed for any of the other clusters of dignitaries nearby. He was making his way toward her. Whispers rustled from behind her, but as he came to a stop, so tantalizingly close, the whispers died. The whole scene should have felt silly, Ann-Sophie told herself, straight out of some teenage drama made for television, but it didn't. It felt breathtakingly real.

Then Alessandro smiled, letting his eyes graze over the others before settling on her again. "Good evening."

Just his voice, low and seductive, made her shiver. A murmur of greetings rippled behind her, but Alessandro's gaze stayed on Ann-Sophie. "Would you care to dance?"

She should say no. Though no rules prohibited their dancing, it felt so brazen. So excessive. But her body didn't care. It reacted with a jolt of giddy desire that scorched her brain of all rational thought and left her with a jumbled rush of sensations. Her silk dress brushed against her skin, making her aware of all the places she wanted his hands. On her hips. On her breasts. Between her legs. The heat from his dark eyes washed over her body, drenching her in desire.

Out of the corner of her eye, Monique's gaze bore into her, a mix of confusion and accusation. But Ann-Sophie ignored the twinge of guilt, telling herself it didn't matter right now, not when that familiar rush of joy ran through her limbs.

"I'm not much of a dancer," she said, repeating the excuse she had given a more appropriate partner not ten minutes ago.

Alessandro's smile was hot and intimate, despite the fact that they were very much not alone. "Thankfully, the dance police have gone home."

If he hadn't made her laugh, maybe she would have ignored the heat that washed over her when the Carandini twin famous for his short-lived flings had sidled up to her at the empty bar on her first night in Nice. But his laughably outrageous flirting had included questions about her flawless Italian, and somehow she had found herself trading anecdotes about language blunders, hers mostly, from adventures with her mother, and his, compliments of a Swiss boarding school and a Saudi girlfriend.

Her first night with Alessandro had unfolded so naturally that when the conversation had meandered into more intimate topics, the intensity of her desire surprised her. After a few high-profile affairs, he had a reputation as a satisfying partner, and she had assumed this reputation to be backed by some reality, but she hadn't expected this to feel so…easy. Fun.

This one night of indulgence had proven addictive. When Alessandro let his gaze fall on her, it felt as if he was the sun, and she opened beneath his rays. There had been moments when he had opened for her, or at least it seemed that way. Afterward, she found herself dismissing them, telling herself that the magnetism he exuded was simply an aspect of his famous diplomatic skills, honed for his family's manufacturing empire. She was just getting a very personalized introduction to the skills he used to negotiate deals, to keep onshore factories from closing. His reputation was legendary, particularly the way he had managed to convince CEOs to choose higher-cost options, gambling that the Made in Italy campaign would ultimately pay off in higher earnings. Still, their nights together had felt more singular than that. More private.

Now, as he stood close enough to touch, she was once again drawn in by the way Alessandro could bridge the distance that spanned between them. A distance of life experiences and social position that was far too wide to forget. And yet, his eyes sparkled with amusement, tempting her to forget.

"This feels like a bad idea," she said, as the curious gazes prodded her from every direction.

Alessandro lifted a hand to his heart theatrically. "You wound me with your rejection."

They both knew that these words were just for show. Alessandro never doubted that she would dance with him.

Still, she arched an eyebrow at him. "I should dance with you to save your tender ego?"

He shrugged with an arrogance that was just as real as it was self-mocking. "Is there a better reason?"

"What a charming offer," she said with a little laugh.

But when she reached out to accept the hand he offered, another burst of giddy joy ran through her. She was almost sure she floated onto the dance floor instead of walked, as if the warmth of his large hand was the only thing that tethered her to the ground. Her face was flushed with heat, and she forced herself to keep her eyes on the floor in front of her, away from the prying eyes that certainly watched them from across the room.

"Just follow my lead, *cara*," he said in her ear. The endearment sent a hot lick of desire through her. "I'll take care of the rest."

It was strange that even these words called to her, so unlike what she usually wanted. Guided by her mother, Ann-Sophie had thrived on making her own way in the world. And yet somehow, as she and Alessandro had shifted from flirting to…whatever this was, she had gotten used to him taking charge a bit more. It was a strange feeling she didn't want to think about too much. So she didn't.

Instead, she turned to face him. She placed her free hand on his muscular shoulder, and the heat of his skin through his shirt seemed to feed the heat that was building inside her. Someone had opened the French doors onto the patio, and the evening air wafted in, redolent with flowers. He slipped his hand around her waist and coaxed her close enough to see hints of circles under his eyes, even in the dim evening light.

"Our sleepless nights are starting to show," she said, brushing her fingers over his sharp cheekbone. This gave her a little thrill, that she might have the power to influence this godlike man.

He flashed her a wicked smile. "Do I need to take you to bed and teach you some manners?"

She laughed, and a surge of happiness coursed through her, one she knew she should suppress. They were still here, in the ballroom.

"I thought we only did this under the cover of darkness," she said. It was better for both of them not to give the impression of distraction at these high-stakes meetings. Now that the meetings were over, it mattered much less, though there would still be speculation.

He pulled back a little and eyed her with amusement. "You were looking at me across the room as though you were making late-night plans for us. I just had to hear what they were."

She noted that he did not ask if she wanted to spend this last night together. He assumed. This may have rubbed her the wrong way if their future was more certain, but tonight, she only felt a surge of anticipation.

"I'm still not sure this is wise," she said as they began to spin their way around past the crown prince and princess of Norway.

The ever-present humor lit up his face. "No one would accuse me of being guided by wisdom, Ann-Sophie."

"Nor I, it seems," she said. "At least not this week."

He leaned forward, so his lips brushed against the sensitive rim of her ear. "I wager that these people around us see an incorrigible playboy who found an intriguing woman to dance with. That's all."

It was difficult to concentrate on his words as memories exploded inside her mind. The sound of his whisper in her ear triggered an image of Alessandro, naked in the bed over her as he whispered the sweetest, softest endearments in her ear, driving her crazy, until she shattered.

"No one knows about our nights together, *cara*," he whispered, the caress of his low voice sending another hot lick of desire through her. "They might wonder, but no one will ever know."

The words were supposed to be a comfort, but Ann-Sophie could not ignore their bitter aftertaste. They reminded her of the truth. No one would know because what they had was not real. After tonight, their affair was over. She had entered the entanglement with no illusions of a future, and yet, as she felt his hard, thick muscles more under her hands, so overtly masculine under his tailored shirt, she knew she had been lying to herself. She wasn't ready to let this end.

Alessandro had not planned to cross this room in front of business colleagues and gossipmongers to ask Ann-Sophie to dance. He had planned to wait until the festivities were winding down before he made his way up to her room for one last night of indulgence. But there had been something in the way the man standing a few meters away from her had looked at her. It had rubbed him the wrong way. He had watched the man approach Ann-Sophie, watched his frown when he turned away, and watched the man's frown as he continued to look at her again.

Alessandro was aware that he could be constructing a narrative out of nothing, and yet he felt obligated to act on it. So he had crossed the room for her sake, he told himself, to make clear that this man was out of her league. Yes, there was an arrogance behind this string of thoughts, but that didn't make them false. Alessandro knew his value and his position in life as well as anyone. And right now, he was enjoying every privilege this position allowed him. He was holding Ann-Sophie, and the brush of her soft curves against his body tempted him to forget this last night of diplomatic alliances and enjoy the startlingly explosive chemistry between them.

"I seem to be having my Cinderella moment," she said, and her tone suggested that she wasn't sure how she felt about it.

"Cinderella returned to her old life at midnight, if I

remember correctly," he said, checking his nonexistent watch. "You left me with no choice. I needed a place on your dance card before this lovely dress turns to rags."

He used this as an excuse to move his hand over the soft curves of her hip. Under his fingers, her red dress washed over her body in a ripple of whisper-thin silk. It was as if he was almost touching her skin, but almost was never enough. He told himself that this craving he felt was just chemistry. Really, really good chemistry.

There were many things Alessandro had learned to close himself off to over the years, but he had found that he did not need to deny the bottomless ache inside him, as long as he dressed it with humor. In every other part of his life, he exercised control. But he allowed the pull of attraction to feed the hunger inside him. Though there were times that this lack of restraint may have suggested an intimacy that hinted at something more, his reputation spoke for itself. Alessandro never thought about the future when he was in the middle of one of these flings because there was no future. Ever.

"I threw away my dance card when the interpreter from Poland invited me onto the floor," she said, and he could sense her smile, even with his eyes closed, his lips so close to her skin. "He is likely judging me at this very moment for my slight."

She said all of this lightly, in that playful tone they communicated in, signaling that she understood that nothing between them should be taken too seriously, but the words still triggered something inside him that he might have called jealousy. That couldn't be right. Still, there had been moments over this week that had felt…different. He could ignore these strange stirrings, he told himself, because tomorrow she would be his past. The affair with Ann-Sophie would end no differently than the others, even if he didn't feel ready to let her go in the same way as he usually did.

"Show me who my competition is, and I will call him out, tomorrow at dawn."

"On the cruel, dusty streets of Nice?" Ann-Sophie's laugh soothed some of the tension inside. "You aristocrats have a reputation for letting others do their dirty work."

She said the word *aristocrats* in a tone that could have been reverence or mockery. Probably a bit of both. He didn't point out that he was not, in fact, an actual aristocrat, though his family had more money than most aristocrats these days. Instead, he said, "I make an exception when it comes to a woman's honor."

"How principled of you." This time, her tone definitely leaned toward mockery. "It's unfortunate that I will be at the airport when all the excitement takes place. I hate to miss it."

There it was, that little waver in her voice. He had heard it the past night, too, when she had made a passing comment about tonight's event, when she had uttered the words *last day.* And one of those moments that felt so *different* had stretched out between them, like a strange, sweet hunger that had gnawed at him.

He had, of course, dismissed it. There were plenty of reasons their connection felt a bit…intense at times. For example, the circumstances were somewhat different this time. For the duration of these affairs, Alessandro had always eased his conscience with the knowledge that the women came to him, not the other way around. They willingly entered into an arrangement with him, knowing the reputation he had clearly established for attachments that were sizzling, satisfying and short-lived. As a rule, he was never to seek out a woman. Alessandro had broken this rule with Ann-Sophie. Even that first night, when he crossed the empty bar and sat next to her, a sense of foreboding had warned him away. He didn't want to think too carefully about why he hadn't ignored it.

There was something so artless and unselfconscious about her, so much the opposite from the way he kept himself strictly under control. As if she didn't feel the weight of expectations on her shoulders. On that first night he had entered the quiet bar around the corner from the hotel to get away from the wariness he couldn't seem to shake when he spent too much time around Massimo and his new wife. But the moment he had sat on the barstool in the corner, next to Ann-Sophie, he wanted her. Craved her enough to set aside the warning signals and pursue her.

Inexplicably, that feeling had grown over the week, not fizzled out. Right now, in the flickering candlelight of the ballroom, he wanted to touch her in a way that might have rattled him if the end of this affair wasn't so clearly in sight. He wanted to run his fingers over her soft skin right here, in front of every business associate that mattered. Dancing with any other woman tonight seemed impossible, and the idea of seeing her dance with indolent royalty and ruthless businessmen, let alone a colleague who might know parts of her that Alessandro hadn't yet learned… It was a vision he put out of his head. Tomorrow he would let Ann-Sophie go, but tonight she was still his.

She shifted under his touch. "You are confident you will win this duel?"

"Of course, I will," he answered smoothly. "If for no other reason, in addition to defending your honor, my demise would mean my brother would single-handedly control our family's fortune. You must have heard talk of the competitive nature of our relationship."

She laughed at this misleading truth. Leaving his brother alone was the last thing he wanted to do, but it had nothing to do with competition. At fifteen, he had been on a path to destruction at the latest boarding school his parents had shipped them off to. Reading and dyslexia weren't a good match, even for someone willing to put in the hard work of that uphill battle. That wasn't Alessandro. Instead, he turned to other distractions, and when his reckless fights had gotten them both kicked out, Massimo stood by his side. They never talked about the period of their lives, when Alessandro's emotions had gotten so out of hand. Massimo, too, had watched their parents' all-consuming relationship, but while his brother had turned inward, Alessandro had shifted into all-out rebellion. He had let his anger and frustration with the things he could not change control him, and that had almost taken down both him, and his brother with him. The poisonous feelings had controlled him until he had turned off that part of himself. It had been the only way to stop the destruction. He would never, ever make Massimo pay for his own sins again.

If Ann-Sophie detected any of the intensity of the responses he was having, she didn't let on. He was grateful for that, he told himself.

"Of course, you will win the duel, as men like you always do," she said lightly, though the humor in her voice had a bite to it. "And then you will return to Milan and bask in the riches of your newfound deals this week."

It was only the vaguest reference to the future, but this comment brushed up against his rule to never speak about the past or the future. His affairs were suspended in a present of mutually satisfying indulgence. When it ended, he left all of it behind. And yet, this week, he had found his conversations with Ann-Sophie drifting outside these boundaries.

He knew he had to cut off this topic, so he indulged Ann-Sophie's question with an answer that diverted her attention. "I will do my celebrating at my flat in Milan, while my brother and his wife will leave for a remote fjord in Norway, which I have been told has many appeals."

"You have never been there?"

Alessandro shook his head. "I prefer more predictable weather."

In truth, Catarina and Massimo had been so caught up in their arranged-marriage-turned-love-match that he had spent very little time with them, beyond cursory meetings and formal gatherings. Alessandro was pleased that his uncompromising brother appeared to be happily married, but it baffled him to see how the relationship had changed his brother, who let so few people inside of the hard exterior he had forged early in life.

In a twist of irony, it was Alessandro himself who had made the winning arguments for his brother's marriage, an idea that Massimo only reluctantly accepted. At the time, a marriage of convenience had seemed to be the wisest course of action, as, unlike Alessandro, his brother had never struggled with keeping his emotions under control and would therefore withstand any weakness that marriage could trigger. However, seeing the way Massimo visibly softened around Catarina had shaken Alessandro, awakening echoes of feelings that were better to remained buried.

So Alessandro had stayed away. At first, his brother had not noted the rift, too caught up in his newly discovered romance. But after months of Alessandro's excuses about why he could not meet for dinner or an evening in their flat, Massimo had confronted him.

"You are avoiding me," his brother had said with his usual stark directness that bordered on harshness. "Explain."

"It seems that falling in love truly does make a person detached from reality. I wouldn't have believed it would happen to you, but…" He ended this with a shrug. He was so good at deflecting emotional traps that even Massimo believed him. At times, a part of him wished these deceptions didn't work as well.

But his brother's features had softened, and he gave a nod, as if Massimo himself had agreed with Alessandro's assessment that love detached him from reality. "I just don't want Catarina to think that this is about her."

Alessandro had looked his brother in the eye and told him it wasn't, because that was the truth. It wasn't her. The problem was the way he was watching his brother change before his eyes. It stirred up a reluctant admiration but also an inexplicable discomfort he didn't want to think about. His parents' relationship may not have warped Massimo, but the anger it triggered in Alessandro was a poison inside him that should never be allowed to rise up again.

Though his brother had found himself carried away by his marriage, Alessandro could never let himself fall into that same trap. He reminded himself that he was under control, despite moments of unsettling intimacy the nights with Ann-Sophie had triggered. There was no tomorrow for them. There was only this dance and the heat of her skin under his hands and her soft, lush body pressed against his. There was tonight, and he would spend it in her now-familiar hotel room, surrounded with wine and decadent desserts, with the moon sparkling on the ocean below. They would talk and eat and lie naked, her body against his, and he would get his fill of satisfying Ann-Sophie, over and over.

When she spoke again, her voice was airy. As if none of this weighed on her. "Surely you must have visited the Nordic countries before?"

"Occasionally. But our company has only started to expand to the region, and my brother prefers to be the one who travels there these days," he said, and then, before he could think to resist, he disturbed his careful boundary between now and their lives outside of this hotel. “And you will return to your apartment and recover from the demands of all of us self-important clients?”

“I am the mediator of ideas. I’d rather like it that way,” she said, maybe too brightly.

Alessandro found this comment frustratingly guarded. “Surely you must want to use your own voice. I, for example, have been enjoying it immensely this week.”

Ann-Sophie laughed. “They pay me a premium to keep my own thoughts—as well as theirs—to myself.”

The idea didn’t sit well with him, but her hair brushed against his cheek, and he let that sensation distract him. They danced in silence, and he told himself everything was right, the way it should be.

“I will travel to Milan now and then in the coming months,” she said after a moment. There was a hesitation in her voice, an uncertain catch in her breath, and Alessandro knew without a doubt that she was about to tread into forbidden territory. She was opening the topic of the future. He had, of course, encountered this problem before, but instead of shifting the conversation, the way he always did, he was overwhelmed by a vision of her in his own bed. Maybe this vision would have been less disturbing if it had been of her soft cries as he pleasured her, the hard thrusts as he took them both to ecstasy. Then he could have simply written it off as lust. But the image in his mind was of Ann-Sophie sitting on his bed, cross-legged, with the morning light shining in her hair like a halo. She was drinking a cappuccino and laughing. It was startlingly, horrifyingly domestic.

But the time to be to take control and redirect the conversation had passed because she was speaking again.

"I was thinking it might be fun to meet up again. You know, have dinner or just..." She shrugged in that carefree way she had. "Do whatever we feel like doing."

A jumbled mess of emotions bombarded him, so ominous that the only thing Alessandro could think to do was shut them down. Shut *her* down.

"We have no future, Ann-Sophie." He told himself he had kept his voice under remarkable control, considering the torrent of stirrings that were seeping through the cracks of his hard-earned equanimity. He could not let them through. He had buried all these emotions long ago. The alternative was to let them erupt, the way they had all those years ago. The way his parents still spread their poison.

Ann-Sophie's eyes widened, and her forehead creased in a vulnerable sort of confusion that unsettled him further. He was making this worse. The smile that slid from her face told him his voice had not been nearly as moderated as he had planned.

The music was still playing, but she had stopped swaying, and Alessandro was keenly aware of the way they were standing in the middle of the ballroom. He watched the hurt slash across her face and had the nagging feeling that this was taking a distinctively bad turn. He had the baffling urge to walk back on his declaration, a reaction that released another jumble of emotions, this one more disturbing than the last.

He had to get the situation under control. This was not the first time he had divested someone of their impression that a future between them was possible, and it would not be the last. He had no choice but to go forward. But as Ann-Sophie blinked up at him, he inexplicably found himself wondering whether there was another path. Then anger washed over her face, and the thought was gone.

"My mistake," she said, her voice cool.

She stepped back and he fisted his hands, keeping himself still. Ann-Sophie's eyes were filled with accusations, but she gave him an exaggerated curtsy and a smile that could only be called mocking.

"I would say it was a pleasure to meet you, but I'm currently reassessing that," she said, her voice now hard as stone. "I'd say I hope to see you again, but that would definitely be a lie."

Then she lifted her chin and turned away, leaving him in the middle of the dance floor.

CHAPTER TWO

Seven months later

"THE GOOD NEWS is that your baby is doing well."

Dr. Azzizi's smile was supposed to be comforting, but Ann-Sophie felt far from reassured. Whenever someone started a conversation with "the good news," nothing good came after that.

Ann-Sophie tried to block that thought out and simply focus on the message. Her baby was fine. The cramping that had convinced her to take a cab directly from the airport to her doctor's office was not an emergency. She was not suffering from a miscarriage, nor was she experiencing signs of early delivery. A little pocket of relief formed amid the billowing clouds of worry in her brain. At least that was one worry to cross off the endless list of pregnancy concerns. Ann-Sophie pasted on a smile for the doctor and tried to adjust the blue gown that curved around her growing belly. Then she took a deep breath and braced herself for the next step of this discussion. "What's the bad news?"

"Your blood pressure is still too high." Dr. Azzizi's eyes were sympathetic, but Ann-Sophie was almost sure her blood pressure had just spiked higher. After the first high reading two months ago, she had taken a monitor home with her and discovered that, in the comfort of her apartment, her blood pressure was in the normal range. However, the moment she left for a work trip, the numbers went up and stayed up. This wasn't exactly a surprise. She had always thrived on the excitement of travel and high-pressure meetings. Unfortunately, the baby didn't, so she had limited herself to shorter trips, and in another month, she would have to stop altogether. Which was stressful, too.

"There's just been so much to do," she said. "And my life is going to change so much after the baby..."

She was still trying to get her head around taking care of a newborn *by herself*, let alone imagining how she would work once maternity leave was over. Currently, during a busy month, she spent more weeks traveling than at home. But she couldn't just...leave a baby for days. Would she have to leave her job instead? And who would employ an interpreter who didn't travel?

Ann-Sophie took a deep breath. Those had all been tomorrow's problems. Today's problem was how to handle the stress of travel. She had tried everything to bring down her blood pressure, starting with more frequent walks and cutting out salt, then working her way up to strict bedtimes...all of which were hard to stick to while traveling. Today, for example, she had woken up in Milan before sunrise after the unexpected extension of the previous day's meeting, instead of catching up on the sleep she had lost this week, as she had planned. This was the kind of schedule crunch that meant that, despite increased interventions, her blood pressure at work kept ticking up. This increasing stress was probably why, when the meeting let out early this morning, she had found herself wandering by the Carandini Corporation's head office before she caught her flight back to Stockholm. Because the visit made no rational sense.

"I've been doing everything you told me to," she told the doctor. "Yoga in the morning, plenty of water…"

"I believe you," said Dr. Azzizi. "But sometimes our bodies don't respond as well as we'd like them to. Your job makes a lot of demands on you. Which is why I'm highly recommending that you go out early on medical leave."

Ann-Sophie blinked at the doctor. "What do you mean?"

"Starting as soon as possible," she said as she typed a note into her computer.

Ann-Sophie gaped at her. "I can't just leave my job."

She was already stressed about fitting in all her commitments before her maternity leave began. This was worse. The thought made her want to curl up on the cold, vinyl exam table and take a nap. Or do something to make this situation go away.

Dr. Azzizi finished typing, and when she looked back up, her smile had faded. "I understand that this will be difficult. You will, of course, be eligible for your full pay because it is medically necessary, but I understand that these situations can be tricky."

Ann-Sophie wondered if her doctor could see the

scope of what she was asking. If she did, it didn't change her mind.

"It is my strong recommendation that you do this now, before the situation becomes more serious. Right now, your at-home measurements indicate you can almost certainly reduce your blood pressure with a less stressful lifestyle. But if you wait, both you and your baby can find yourselves in a much different situation."

The words rattled through Ann-Sophie's body ominously, making her shiver.

"But I feel fine," she protested weakly.

The doctor raised her eyebrows.

"Fine-ish?" she amended.

But even that was an exaggeration. First, there had been the bouts of morning sickness, and as her belly grew, her feet tended to be sore and swollen at the end of the day. That was just the beginning of the list. Still, the last thing she needed was lots of free time to worry more often. "It's just that my body doesn't feel like I need rest."

"You should definitely stay active," said the doctor. "Swim, walk, stretch. It's the stress that needs to change, and after two months of modifying everything else, we're down to the last option. You need to stop traveling for work."

"But I love to travel," Ann-Sophie whispered.

Exploring new places was one of her very favorite things about her job, and now, her last month of it was gone. When was the next time she could start her morning at a window seat in a new coffee shop with a pastry and her journal? When the baby turned eighteen?

Of course, she knew these sacrifices were coming and was willing to make them. She just didn't think they would come so soon. So suddenly.

The doctor furrowed her brow. "You could take a vacation instead. Maybe a solo retreat or go with a friend?"

Ann-Sophie let out a sigh. On her first visit with the midwife at *Barnavårdscentralen*, she was asked to check one of the two boxes on the form she had filled out: single or partnered? Ann-Sophie hadn't hesitated. She'd checked off *single* quickly and deliberately, as if she, like her mother, had made a conscious decision to have a baby without a partner.

Because who wanted a partner who, surrounded by their colleagues, would clarify that their nights together were essentially meaningless sex? She had made the mistake of believing her week with Alessandro had transcended their differences. But in the middle of that opulent ballroom, he had exposed the truth: He could yank that feeling from under her feet at any time. She had felt silly and small. Less than. And it triggered all her leftover feelings from her nonrelationship with her father, feelings she absolutely would not dwell on now, when she had her own child. Because she would never allow this child to feel less than. Unwanted. Abandoned. Not worth their parent's time.

Apparently, Alessandro had been so committed to the message he delivered in the ballroom scene that he decided a further step was necessary. Adding insult to injury, he *blocked her number.* The fact that this move still hurt to think about was yet another source of frustration. What happened to the woman who had loved her single life, surrounded by friends and free to travel, explore and follow her whims and curiosities?

"I'll ask some friends if they're free," she said, though she knew none of them could pick up and leave for a spontaneous trip now, in early September, right after the summer holidays.

"You will be doing both yourself and your baby a favor," said Dr. Azzizi, but Ann-Sophie barely heard her.

As she walked out the door of the office with the printout of her doctor's orders in one hand and her carry-on suitcase in the other, she reminded herself that this phase would pass. Fall had arrived in Stockholm, and a cold gust of wind blew through the narrow streets as she walked to the main office of Swedish Connection Interpreting Services. Ann-Sophie had no memory of what she said to the head of human resources when she wandered into the office. All she remembered was the sympathetic smile Birgitta had given her when she said, "Don't worry. We'll take care of this. Just get some rest, and we'll message you with any questions."

Don't worry? Ann-Sophie had to bite back a humorless laugh.

And just like that, all her clients were reassigned. She was free. Very free and very alone. And now that the buffer of work and travel was gone, she was suddenly terrified. She was having a baby *alone*. And the reality of this very uncertain future was starting today.

Her heart thumped harder in her chest, and she reminded herself to calm down. No freaking out in the middle of the street. Having a baby on her own had upsides, she told herself. She and the little one would make their own family. Soon, she would have a baby to love and care for. This strange pang of loneliness would go away.

She mused that this rudderless feeling was hormones.

As she walked through the crowds at Odenplan, Ann-Sophie dialed her mother, but the call went straight to voice mail. Which was unsurprising, as her mother's journalism assignments often took her far beyond the reaches of mobile-phone services. Ann-Sophie searched her memory for where her mother was supposed to be, but pregnancy brain seemed to have stolen these details, so she left a message, hoping her mother would call back in the evening, when she had more time. Margarita Svensson had not raised a needy child. Ann-Sophie admired her mother, and any wish for a more conventional upbringing had long ago died. But just this once, she wanted to dial her mother's number and hear her voice. Just that thought triggered a wave a guilt. Her mother had already given up too much for her, including the man she loved. Ann-Sophie would never ask for more.

Instead of dwelling on this, she sent messages to three friends, proposing weekend getaways. Two messaged back immediately.

Linnea: Sorry! Lena has a ballet recital Saturday afternoon. Call you later!

Helena: Working over the weekend. :(Hope you're well!

Ann-Sophie ducked into a bakery for her second treat of the day, then headed toward her flat in Vasastan. It wasn't until she was on the familiar back streets of her neighborhood that her mind wandered back to Alessandro.

Ann-Sophie's face still flushed with humiliation when she remembered that last night in Nice. She had been imagining scenarios for her next visit, and he had unquestionably moved on. She was so careful with men, so conscious of her still-tender wounds about being abandoned, but something about the intimacy of their connection that week had made her think this was different. At the very least, he could have rejected her with a little more grace. But she had clearly been wrong about him.

The humiliation turned to alarm two weeks later when she calculated that she had missed her period. Multiple tests confirmed what her body sensed: She was pregnant. Though she always had wanted a child or two someday, the *someday* she had imagined was much further in the future. And she had taken it for granted that she would do this together with a partner she loved. But her mother's words came through shortly after, words about Ann-Sophie's own unexpected appearance in her mother's life: "It's never the right time for a baby. If you want a child, you make it the right time."

So Ann-Sophie had made the decision. She was having a baby. Despite their less-than-desirable parting, she decided to call Alessandro, just to inform him. Which was how she discovered he had blocked her number. Ann-Sophie remembered the sinking feeling when the words flashed across the screen of her mobile. Still, after a few weeks of wallowing, she had swallowed her pride for the baby's sake and tried again, this time sending a discreet email: I have something important we need to discuss. Please call me.

He, of course, ignored it.

She had contemplated leaving a very detailed message with the receptionist in his office, a kind of revenge that exposed his dirty laundry for those he worked with. But as satisfying as the idea sounded, she couldn't do it. She was carrying this man's child, and no matter how humiliated and frustrated she was, they would have this baby between them for their entire lives. The idea triggered a strange rustle of feelings inside that she refused to contemplate, so she had focused on the baby, leaving the situation with Alessandro for later. She would find a way to tell him before the baby came. She was just…working her way up to it.

With each work trip to Milan, the guilt of not telling him weighed a little heavier. She *and Alessandro* had created a baby. And he still had no idea. Though the Carandini family business had nothing to do with her visit, somehow she had still expected to cross paths with Alessandro. She had expected that the opportunity to tell him would simply present itself. Fate had brought them together seven months ago. Wouldn't it bring them together again?

When fate didn't cooperate, she took matters into her own hands and looked up the address of his office. If a detailed phone message was petty revenge, showing up to his office seven months pregnant was positively wicked. And incredibly tempting. She had stood on the sidewalk outside the sleek, modern building in the center of the city, gathering her nerves as guilt warred with unease. What if she confronted him, and he walked away, just like her father did?

Ann-Sophie could not make herself enter the building. At one point, she had thought she'd seen a glimpse of Alessandro through the glass, but if it was, in fact, him, he had turned back the moment he saw her. In the end, nothing had come of the visit aside from higher blood pressure. Next time, she told herself. Maybe there was a chance he would welcome a baby. Maybe every aspect of her baby's life didn't have to depend on her. In truth, she was overwhelmed, daunted by the task of caring for this tiny, helpless being by herself, and she wanted her baby to be welcomed into the world with love, not stress. For the next two months, she needed to do everything in her power to make sure of it… which meant figuring out how to handle the situation with Alessandro.

But before she could think about that mess, she was starving. Again. So hungry that she was clearly hallucinating because the man standing outside her building looked a lot like…

No. It couldn't be.

Because there, in front of her tall, stone building, stood Alessandro Carandini. There was a starkness to him she hadn't noticed before. His thick, glossy hair was clipped shorter than it had been seven months ago, and the cut of his suit accentuated his wide shoulders, making him look even taller than she remembered. But his eyes were the same, and they triggered sensations from seven months ago she had buried. Heat swept through her, and her swollen breasts tingled and ached. Her body *knew* him. A hot rush of desire mixed with that uneasy giddiness she had refused to think about before. But as Alessandro came into undeniable focus, heat skittered through her body, and she could no longer push the awareness away. This feeling was hope. And for one, heart-stopping moment, he looked at her as if everything in the world had been made right again.

Before Ann-Sophie had time to think through practical questions, like what was he doing here, in front of her apartment building, his gaze drifted down to her belly. Ann-Sophie's heart thudded in her chest as she caught unmistakable desire glittering in his gaze. But the desire immediately disappeared, and his eyes narrowed. He took a step forward, then another, and with each step, his expression turned harder. By the time he towered over her, he looked far from the charming aristocrat she had spent that one glorious week in Nice with. Instead, he looked stunned. And angry.

Lush. Ripe. The sensations fueled by these words roared through Alessandro's body. He stared at Ann-Sophie, trying to contain the racket of emotions that thundered through him. She was *pregnant*. He felt an overwhelming urge to reach for her, to touch her, to feed the hunger that raged inside him. But he gritted his teeth and focused on the other reactions that vied for his attention. Like shock. And outrage. He clung to them, letting them blossom until they quieted the ever-present desire for her that still dogged him, even seven months later. It was this combination of shock and outrage that had spurred this unexpected trip to Stockholm, from the moment his brother had walked into his office and declared that he was almost sure he had seen Ann-Sophie outside their building.

"And she looked..." Massimo, who never found himself at a loss of words, often to Alessandro's dismay, hesitated.

"What is it?" Alessandro's patience had been chronically short in recent months, and this topic wasn't helping. His brother raised an eyebrow, and Alessandro was forced to remember how he had mocked Massimo not so long ago about his brother's sudden turns of temper when Catarina had fled. But this situation was completely different. He gave Massimo a tight smile. "How did she look?"

Massimo frowned, and warning signals exploded in Alessandro's mind. "Her belly looked a bit rounder."

It was as if Alessandro's entire body went numb. He didn't realize he was walking until he was out the door. He found himself in the elevator, glaring impatiently as the floors ticked down until he finally arrived at street level. But Ann-Sophie was nowhere. His assistant searched every hotel until he found the place were she was staying, just three blocks from his office. Except she had already checked out. Still, the fact that she had been there, so close, suggested Massimo had not been mistaken about whom he had seen, though surely his brother was wrong about... Alessandro didn't even want to think about why she might be "rounder."

It implied the unthinkable.

It implied the thing that should never, ever happen.

For the last seven months, he had been haunted by their week together, but Alessandro had sworn to himself that he would never see Ann-Sophie again. The lingering ache for her was the price he was paying for the way he had let his control slip for one, short moment on the dance floor, he told himself. But if she was… No, he would not let himself think about it until he had confirmation.

Which meant he needed to go directly to her apartment and clear up this situation.

"You could be waiting outside her apartment for days," his brother had said over the phone as Alessandro sped toward the airport. "To think it wasn't so long ago that you were the one telling me that I was not acting rational."

"This is not the same," he growled at his brother.

"Not at all," Massimo had replied all too easily. "Because I was actually engaged to the woman I was pursuing. Whereas you are quite far from that."

Somewhere over Europe, in the privacy of his jet, where he could think more rationally, Alessandro had reassured himself that she couldn't be…rounder. Instead, he found himself planning to see her again. If his brother had been mistaken, and he found himself face-to-face with Ann-Sophie, close enough to touch, he would make an excuse for being in town and apologize for his unfortunate behavior. Naturally, she would forgive him. This would soothe both the unsettling memory of their last night together and, if all went as planned, satisfy the desire that had plagued him, and finally put it to rest.

And if his brother was right? Alessandro had turned to stare out at the clouds, trying not to think about that possibility.

But now, as he stood on this narrow street, under the tempestuous Stockholm sky, the evidence in front of him was irrefutable. Ann-Sophie was standing in front of him with a rolling suitcase in tow, and the word *round* didn't begin to capture her belly. *Lush. Ripe.* Those words continued to echo inside him, over and over, despite the fact that here on the street, he could only see a hint of this new development under her outer layers. Seven months of repressing her voice, her laugh, the way her body seemed to be made especially for him—everything came back so viscerally. The hints of new curves under her shawl made his hands clench with the need to touch her in all the ways he shouldn't. Because the hunger that gnawed inside him was mixed with the jumble of emotions he had spent his adulthood shutting off.

He glared at her belly incredulously, focusing on the fact that she hadn't said a word about this situation to him.

"You are pregnant." The words were an accusation that he flung at her, and for a moment she looked as if he had slapped her. Hurt and betrayal flashed across her face, and he hated the way it wrenched at him. Then her eyes narrowed.

"How very observant of you." She tilted her head a little. "You know, I remember you as significantly more charming. Funnier. At least until those last moments on the dance floor."

And he remembered her as easygoing. The last seven months of being pregnant on her own appeared to have given her teeth. Or maybe just the desire to use them on him.

"Is it my child?"

She rolled her eyes, as if this much was obvious.

"How did this happen?"

"My grade four teacher was pretty clear about the process, but maybe your fancy boarding schools left these details vague?"

He glared at her. "We used condoms."

"Most of the time. I've had seven months to go back over our week. It's definitely possible."

Alessandro's anger and lust flared, intertwining into something far more dangerous as he pictured a few choice moments of carelessness. He had spent the last seven months intentionally *not* going over that week. Now, flashes of their nights came back, feeding the storm clouds gathering in his mind. Building, threatening to unleash their power and envelop everything around him. He narrowed his eyes. "You didn't tell me."

"Did you think that email I sent about 'something important' was a plea for more sex?" She huffed out a sigh. "Never mind. I don't want to know how truly impressive your ego is."

He bit back a snappier response because he had, in fact, thought something quite similar. Instead, he made an attempt to soften his voice. "We need to talk."

She glared at him. He waited. Finally, she broke the silent war with a sigh and a shake of her head.

"Let's go inside," she said, and she didn't wait for his answer.

Alessandro followed her through the front door and into the lobby, with its marble floors and brass letter boxes, as frustrations welled inside him—frustrations he didn't know where to aim. She bypassed the elevator and headed for the stairs, despite the fact that she was pulling a suitcase behind her.

"Why are you walking up?" he demanded. "Shouldn't you be…"

He gestured vaguely to her body as he tried to remember what common wisdom said about what a pregnant woman should do. He was sure it included being careful about, well, everything.

"I'm perfectly capable of walking up stairs." Ann-Sophie gestured to the sign taped next to the brass call button, written in unintelligible Swedish. "Also, the elevator is broken. They're ordering a part, but…"

She shrugged, as if she had long ago accepted this fact and moved on. Again, his frustration bubbled to the surface, pushing aside those dangerous poisons of betrayal and lust.

"I will make sure it is fixed today." At least one problem in this mess had a concrete solution.

The dry humor he remembered flashed across her face. "Of all the problems I have right now, that one doesn't even rank in the top one hundred."

The reference to all her problems raked through him uncomfortably.

"Let me carry your suitcase," he said, just barely holding on to his calm facade. His temper must have shown on his face because her expression softened a little.

"Thank you," she said and handed it to him.

Then she turned around and continued up the stairs as he stewed over this last comment. She said it as if she was *humoring* him. This situation obviously needed some clarifications.

Ann-Sophie climbed the stairs, past the second-floor landing of the spiral staircase, and came to a stop on the landing on the third floor, lit by the overcast sky through the window in the stairwell. She keyed the door, and they stepped into a tiny hallway. The floor was filled with mail and newspapers, and as she bent to pick up everything, her full rear brushed against his thigh. His body stirred again, and Alessandro gritted his teeth. This woman had the power to take over his thoughts and make him act irrationally. It had already happened once, with disastrous consequences, and he could feel how easily it could happen again.

"I'll get the mail," he growled.

Everything he did from this point forward must be strategic, and from the moment he had registered her round belly, partly concealed by the billowy shawl she wore, Alessandro knew immediately what the goal had to be. He would never be a negligent father and treat his child like an inconvenience—or worse—the way his own parents had. And though Alessandro had never envisioned himself as a father, he had very strong ideas about how a child should be raised. He needed a solution that would give him some much-needed control over this…situation. Which required keeping the child and Ann-Sophie close. That's what this strange, possessive urge was about, he told himself. The solution he had in mind did not involve intense emotions. As long as he kept himself under control, he could fix this situation into something that worked. He had succeeded with more delicate negotiations, and he always pursued his interests relentlessly until he was satisfied with the outcome. This would be no different.

He took a moment to evaluate her living conditions, which, on the whole, looked perfectly acceptable, though a little small. The apartment's old wooden floors and high ceilings lined with flourishes marked the building's age, but it had been kept up reasonably well. Alessandro hung his coat on a brass coatrack and followed her into a living room. The walls were white and decorated with a series of paintings that could have been Southeast France or Northwest Italy. The most notable feature was an old-fashioned, floor-to-ceiling stovelike fireplace, freestanding and entirely covered with tile. The rest of the room was decorated in the Scandinavian modern style that one might expect, with a low, white sofa and chairs and an area rug patterned in tan and white. On the whole, the room was tasteful and might have even felt a bit impersonal if not for the books. They were everywhere, in overflowing piles on the bookshelves and scattered on the furniture and the low tables, some bookmarked and others propped open.

Ann-Sophie cleared a book from the armchair and

gestured for him to sit. "I'm putting on the kettle for peppermint tea. Would you like a cup?"

He shook his head. The drink he needed right now was significantly stronger.

She disappeared through the doorway, and he wandered through the room, inspecting the books that lay open, faced down, half-read and abandoned. There were a few in Italian and English that he recognized, but most were in what he assumed was Swedish. Ann-Sophie clearly loved to read, and Alessandro filed this information away for future strategic use. She returned moments later with a tray that held a cup of tea and a plate that held some sort of sugary bun, which she set next to a stack of older-looking books.

"Cinnamon roll?" She glanced longingly at the braided bun. "I split it in half in case you're hungry."

"No, thank you," he said, and he was almost sure he saw a flash of relief.

Ann-Sophie reached for the sweet, giving it a reverent glance before taking a bite. She closed her eyes, and a look of sensual pleasure swept across her face. Alessandro's body reacted immediately, memories mixing with seven months of self-denial in a surge of lust that for one, dangerous moment took over his thoughts with pure need, reckless and desperate.

"Where shall we start?" she asked a moment later with a tight smile. "Perhaps with the way you so succinctly made it clear you wanted nothing to do with me after a week together? And just so there was no uncertainty in your message, you felt it necessary to block my number. Yes, let's start there."

The new bite he had noted was back in her voice, sinking its teeth into him. A few days after their parting, he had found himself inexplicably checking his phone to see if she might have contacted him, despite the way he'd ended their liaison. Finally, he put an end to that impulse by blocking her number. But this was definitely not the time to get into these details.

"Or we could start with the current situation." He gestured to her belly, but he was distracted by the way the pillows under her legs were propped in such a way that suggested she regularly sat like this. Did her feet bother her? Alessandro didn't like the way that possibility sat inside him.

"Fine. Let's start with today," she said. "Why were you waiting outside my building?"

The question narrowed his focus. They were entering negotiation, an area where he excelled. Growing up as the disappointing twin, the troublemaker, it had been implied in every way that he would be the one who would surely bring down the family name his grandfather wanted so desperately to redeem. When he had finally shut off his emotions, he had learned to hone in on his useful skills.

All his adult life, he had talked his way through situations where his father had betrayed every last ounce of trust that people had in the family name. He had succeeded, winning back clients. Armed with the facts, plans and financial nuances Massimo had compiled, he had explained, flattered and negotiated, all with the air that in the end, it didn't matter to him. That they had lists of investors clambering for access if this particular investor turned down their proposal. While his brother was good at numbers, forecasts and all the things that had plagued Alessandro at school, Alessandro knew *people*. He knew how to charm and enthrall, and he carried out each charm offensive with steely resolve because he had sworn that never again would their lives be out of control, the way that they had been during their childhood. So he ignored the questions about how she was fairing that brewed inside and started on this new campaign.

"I came to ask you the very same question," he said, his voice a peak of equanimity. "Just this morning, my brother told me that he saw you in front of our office, looking 'rounder.' I believed that a pregnancy was out of the question because the woman I spent a week with seven months ago had a job that entirely depended on her integrity. So she would never, ever fail to reveal something as important as a baby."

Ann-Sophie swallowed visibly, but her reply was cuttingly polite. "May I refer back to the email I mentioned?"

"Surely you could have tried a bit harder," he said, ignoring the fact that she did, indeed, have a point. "After all, you managed to make it to the doorstep of our office."

Her lips twitched down in displeasure.

"I'm sorry. I should have," she finally whispered.

A rush of cool satisfaction ran through him. He had found a weakness. She felt guilty about withholding this information. So he twisted the knife further.

"But, as my brother has earned my *trust*—" Alessandro slowed on that last word "—I felt it was my duty to verify that he had made some sort of mistake, that my trust in your honesty was not misplaced."

Again, her guarded expression faltered, and again he ignored the twinge of discomfort this reaction brought and focused on the surge of satisfaction of having found a path forward. A path where he was in control. Alessandro told himself that even if he hadn't made it easy for her, she still should have found a way to tell him about the baby.

"But now, I find myself here, having verified that my brother was not, in fact, mistaken. It was I who was so deceived into thinking that I could trust someone who has security clearances," he said, finishing. Then, he waited.

Ann-Sophie was quiet for a long time as she looked out the window. Finally, she turned back to him. "So basically, you came here to scold me?"

Frustration flared inside him, but it was easy to tamp it down this time because he had her exactly where he wanted her.

"Oh, no, *cara*," he said, softening his tone. "I didn't come to scold you. I came to marry you."

CHAPTER THREE

ANN-SOPHIE WAS almost sure her blood pressure had just doubled. Marry notorious playboy Alessandro Carandini? This was the same man who had jettisoned her on the dance floor the moment she mentioned a future encounter, but now, he wanted her to agree to spend the rest of her life with him? For the last seven months, she had been bracing herself for the possibility that he would abandon the child with the kind of callous disinterest her father showed her. The idea of marriage felt like the opposite extreme and just as overwhelming. She was already so overwhelmed that, for one brief moment, the idea of simply giving in and letting Alessandro take care of things on a day like today was tempting.

Hormones, she reminded herself. Hormones were making her feel vulnerable, along with today's unforeseen news from the doctor. Alessandro had caught her at a vulnerable moment. Why else would she invite this man into her living room, listen to his demands for marriage and not kick him out. Her yoga teacher's voice echoed in her head in a loop, chanting *deep, calming breaths...deep, calming breaths.*

"You must be joking," she finally said.

"I assure you I am not. Marriage is the obvious solution to this…" He gestured at her body, currently sprawled across the sofa, as if he had no words for her state. "It is the best way for both of us to put this child first."

"I'm glad you want to put the baby first," she said, keeping her voice even, "but there are many ways to do this without marriage. Like co-parenting, for example."

"From different countries?"

"We'd have a lot of details to work out, but marriage is no different."

He looked, in a word, determined. His strong feelings about marriage were a surprise, considering the fact that he was the last person anyone would associate with marriage. Ann-Sophie suspected she wasn't getting the whole story about why. Maybe the best way forward was attempting to understand these motivations so she could work out a compromise that worked for both her and the baby.

But before she could figure out an approach, Alessandro distracted her with a lazy smile. "It could be mutually satisfying."

The most maddening thing was how these words in his smooth, low voice still sent a shiver of desire through her. This was the tone he had used in the bedroom for much more pleasurable reasons. Ann-Sophie had thought these feelings had turned off when the uncompromising pink line of the pregnancy test had stared up at her. But the moment his eyes raked down her body, it was as if her blood began to sing. Her body tingled as if ready and waiting for the promise his smile suggested. She was still so vulnerable to his seduction.

To him.

The ache that reached beyond attraction was even more dangerous. Which was why she absolutely should not think about it. She could never let that influence her decisions, not when she was deciding for two.

"But marriage is between *us*," she said slowly. "Why should I say yes to spending the rest of my life with you?"

Alessandro still wore that lazy, seductive smile, the one he had given her back in Nice, the one that made her forget their very different lives and made her dream. But this time, it felt as if he was toying with her body's reactions, using them against her while he remained totally under control. All the frustration she had seen when he glared at her in the front of her building had dissolved, and in its place, she felt a will of steel behind his indolent smile. Was this hardness new, or had it been there the whole time, carefully hidden when she posed no threat to his world order? She had been an insignificant fling—one of many, forgettable, she reminded herself. Insignificant enough to *block her calls.*

"A marriage would mean that you would have my wealth at your disposal," he said with a wave of his hand, as if he was some sort of king that granted his subject's wishes, according to his whims. "This could allow for an upgrade in your living situation, for example. You will not have to work, nor will our child want for anything. You will be free to travel, which you mentioned you'd love to do more of. In fact, you can spend your whole life traveling."

Maybe another day this offer wouldn't have tempted her, but after the news that her world was suddenly getting a lot smaller, travel without limits sounded heavenly. Her mother's words came back to her. *You must learn to tell the difference between wants and needs,* älskling. Travel was a want. Setting up a life for the baby was a need. She couldn't let her own wants get in the way.

Deep, calming breaths. The steel will she heard underneath his comments suggested that even if she dismissed him from her apartment, this discussion was not going away. He was father of the baby she was carrying, which demanded a degree of negotiation, no matter what their marital status was.

His gaze raked over her body, and that unmistakable heat in his eyes made her breasts feel fuller, heavier. She tried to ignore it. "What if I am not swayed by what your wealth can do for me?"

"Maybe you should experience it before you so quickly reject the benefits," Alessandro answered mildly.

"Like endless vacations?" She gave him a polite smile and pretended he was a client to be humored. "And what would you be doing as I took these trips to spas and exclusive resorts?"

"Aside from upholding my side of mutual satisfaction," he began, and she recognized the familiar raw desire in his gaze, "I would be working, the same way I work now."

"The same way you were working in Nice? With the nights reserved for affairs like the one that you had with me?" His expression darkened, but Ann-Sophie ignored it. "I suppose that would mean I am also free to gallivant around with other men, so long as I keep it—"

"There will be no extramarital affairs." His voice had turned hard and icy. He swallowed, and some of the easygoing veneer returned—because she was beginning to understand that this was a veneer. "Not on either of our parts."

She looked away, not wanting him to see how relieved she was that at least one of her concerns was off the table. She gathered herself again and gave him what she hoped would pass for an amused smile.

"So I will have plenty of time alone?" she asked. "Just a baby and me? What a relief for a new mother."

He narrowed his eyes at the wryness in her voice. "Resorts are rarely empty, and you may hire nannies or invite friends to stay with you. Or relatives, which I assume you have. You will not be alone."

"My mother is a journalist with a heavy travel schedule, and my father wasn't around, so I can't picture either of them at a spa with me." There was a sharpness in her voice, and Ann-Sophie wasn't sure why she had made that comment. She usually avoided mentioning her father altogether. She glanced at Alessandro, wondering if the comment had simply rolled past him, but to her dismay, he looked deep in thought. Suddenly, she didn't want to be in the middle of this conversation.

"Wealth would mean choices. You could indulge the child in whatever you chose," he finally said.

"An indulged child. What a charming offer," she said. She wanted a family for her child. She wanted her child to be surrounded by the warm love she had always missed when her mother had gone away to some far-flung location. Right now, this was too much to process, so she feigned a conciliatory tone. "I'll consider it."

She wiggled her feet, which were feeling better, then swung her legs around to the floor without fully taking into account the awkwardness and level of effort it took to stand up at this point in her pregnancy. It was embarrassing, really. At work and in public, she took care to sit on chairs that were higher so as never to get stuck. She had expected herself to be one of those pregnancy women who trained for marathons, not the type to get stuck on her sofa like a pill bug. Still, one of the many benefits of living alone was that, in her apartment, she didn't have to give much thought to it. If she ended up rolling around a bit to make it to standing, no one was here to judge. But the effort of getting up from a sofa that sunk as low and comfortably as hers was decidedly ungraceful. And now that she had begun, it was too late to do anything but forge ahead.

Her face flushed as she rocked forward and leaned heavily on the arm of the couch to get up, but before she made it any farther, Alessandro was on his feet, next to her, helping her up with a gentleness that sent a strange tightness through her chest. A part of her wanted to simply give in to him. She was tired of being strong, tired of putting on a smile and telling everyone that she was fine. She wanted this baby badly, but she hadn't expected pregnancy to be quite this tough. Now, she was close to Alessandro, close enough that she couldn't ignore how much she had missed the scent of him. Or the way her breath caught in her throat when his hand came to her cheek. She turned, and his eyes were hooded with unmistakable desire.

"Please do consider all the advantages of my offer," he said, and his husky voice sent a shiver of need through her.

Ann-Sophie drew in an unsteady breath and forced herself to look away from his deep brown eyes. "I'm going to make supper."

He let her go, but instead of taking this as a dismissal, Alessandro followed her through the hallway. Her body felt so alive right now. Alessandro's sudden appearance and promise to whisk her away into a life of luxury was a rush of relief and hope that made her feel vulnerable. After the way he'd left her so abruptly, he was the last person she wanted to see her this way.

She turned into her kitchen, with the table in the breakfast nook on one side and the little balcony that looked out onto the courtyard of her building. She headed for the refrigerator.

"Are you hungry?" she asked. "I haven't been home in a week, so I don't have much to choose from. I was thinking broccoli soup and sandwiches."

"You should be eating—"

Ann-Sophie braced herself for oncoming pearls of wisdom on pregnant women—from the man who was likely the least knowledgeable on this topic in the continent. But he stopped, mid-sentence, and she felt a shift in tension in the room. She turned and found Alessandro looking at the built-in shelves next to the table. Actually, *glaring* was a more accurate description, and she immediately saw what had caught his eye. Her blood-pressure monitor, lying on top of the sheet she used to record the results.

Ann-Sophie crossed the room to snatch the paper away before he could get a closer look at it.

"Is there a problem with your blood pressure?" His tone was even, but she could hear a hint of warning in it.

"Right now?" She tilted her head, as if she had to consider his question. "Yes, in fact. The direction of this conversation is likely shooting up my blood pressure. Thank you for your concern."

She wasn't sure what she expected his response to be. Perhaps an argument or maybe blame, much the way she blamed herself. But he said nothing. He simply stared at her, looking genuinely stunned. Finally, he gestured to the table. "Sit down. I will make supper. Please."

The word *please* rippled through her with a rush of relief in its wake. She tried to muster up a little bit of frustration that he was taking over, but she was tired. The early meeting, the apparently less-than-subtle wander to Alessandro's offices in Milan, the flight, Dr. Azzizi's news and the thought of early maternity leave—it was all just…a lot. She closed her eyes, trying to gather her feelings. Even if she had no interest in marrying a man who had so easily ditched her before, he could make her supper. Especially since the other methods of relaxation he could provide were not a good idea.

So she settled at the table as he watched her, arms crossed, his expression inscrutable. "What are you hungry for?"

She chose to ignore the sexual undertones her exhausted mind was gravitating toward and focused on his actual question. She was always hungry these days, a fickle kind of hunger that demanded everything from bacon-flavored chocolate, to pickles, to wasabi peas. And cinnamon rolls, of course. None of those things could be classified as supper.

"It doesn't matter. Whatever you can make from the ingredients in my bare cupboards," she said.

Alessandro waved off her comment and pulled out his phone, and his side of the conversation suggested the person on the other end of the line was waiting for him nearby. He ordered a list of ingredients that made her mouth water, and she felt more of the tension of the day fall away. It was just a meal, she reminded herself. She hadn't agreed to anything. Definitely not marriage, a demand she still hadn't completely processed.

Why on earth was he interested in getting married? The last thing she wanted to hear about was some antiquated notion of bloodlines. There had been something almost raw in his voice that suggested his real reasons lay closer to the heart. If this man had a heart. After his cold dismissal of her in Nice, she wasn't so sure.

He ended the call and then turned to her. "While we wait, is there anything else you need to tell me? Twins, perhaps?"

"There is only one baby," she said, "though at this point I look like I'm carrying at least two."

"What is the gender?"

"I'm not going to find out," she said, hoping that he could hear that this was not negotiable.

"We will do a paternity test, of course," he continued in a tone that implied that she should be taking notes or doing something to make sure she carried out his wishes to his liking.

"Will we?" She raised her eyebrows. "No one is backing you into this situation. You can walk away at any point."

He opened his mouth as if to reply, then closed it. Frowned.

Ann-Sophie sighed. "There are no other candidates, Alessandro."

"And I should take you at your word?" He gestured to her belly. "You kept this from me for seven months."

She closed her eyes and sighed. "I'm sorry you found out this way. I was going to tell you before the baby came, but I couldn't figure out how."

He raised his eyebrows doubtfully.

She frowned. "I can't change what I did. If you have so little faith in me, then you should probably leave right now. Remember my stress problem?"

Alessandro looked like he had plenty to say on this subject but refrained. As it turned out, high blood pressure was proving to have at least one upside.

He turned to face the counters, and she watched as he familiarized himself with her kitchen, inspecting her utensils and pans. This suggested that he himself was planning to make the meal, which surprised her, considering the fact that he had an army of staff at his disposal to take care of these things for him. But cooking was apparently one of the things he valued, something he had clearly decided not to fully outsource. That thought was a little depressing, considering how quickly he had talked about outsourcing the care of her and the baby to resorts and nannies.

Alessandro's back was to her, and she watched his muscles move under his crisp, white dress shirt, triggering memories of what those muscles felt like under her hands, what it felt like when his arms were around her as he laughed at her stories and kissed her so tenderly. No, it wasn't what his wealth could buy that was the hard to resist. It was the man himself.

By the time Alessandro tossed the pasta with fresh sausage, garlic-sautéed spinach, pine nuts and Parmesan, he was in control of his emotions again. He had been forced to control them after the bombshell of Ann-Sophie's high blood pressure was followed by her comment that suggested that he was, in fact, a current stress factor.

The urge to pressure her was strong, to get her to follow him to the nearest church immediately and get this situation under his full control. Marriage would bring stability to this situation and to their child's life—something he had never had. Right now, he was in no condition to consider what being a father would require of him; he would figure that out when the baby came. Instead, he focused on the way marriage would soothe the volcano of emotions that had been erupting since Massimo had walked into his office this morning.

Guilt, obligation and subtle exercises of power were some of his well-traveled negotiation routes, but these relied on creating increasing stress on the target, a method that was now out of the question. Alessandro needed to drastically reevaluate his approach.

He set the plates of pasta on the table, and she looked at the food with open desire. She took a deep breath of the mingling spices that wafted from the dishes. As she took her first bite, the tension eased from around her eyes.

"You can cook," she said with a hint of surprise, and he noted that her voice had lost a little of its sharpness.

"Of course, I can," he said, waving away the comment. "Meals give us three opportunities every day for pleasure. Why wouldn't I take advantage of them?"

She gave him an amused smile. "Good point."

Was this a negotiation path to marriage, one guided by pleasures? Foods, comforts, luxuries and physical desires… Some combination of these could sway with her.

"I used to cook more often when I stayed with my grandmother during the summers," she said, a little wistfully. Then she gave a little laugh. "A lot of meatballs and boiled potatoes. Not like this."

"I learned to cook from my grandmother, too," he said. She raised an eyebrow, and he raised his hands in protest. "You don't believe me?"

Ann-Sophie shrugged. "I'm just having a hard time picturing it."

"It was an interesting summer," he said darkly.

She rested her fork on her plate and tilted her head, watching him as if she was waiting for him to continue. It brought him back to moments ago, when, reeling from the high-blood-pressure revelation, and struggling to contain yet another surge of emotions, Alessandro had come close to pleading with her. *Please.* That one word had revealed far too much of the raw fear she had triggered, but it had also gotten through to her. The emotions he kept under tight control were another tool he could use, one that clearly got Ann-Sophie's attention. This path was more dangerous, but he would never let himself get out of hand. Never again.

When he didn't continue, she asked, "When are you planning to return to Milan?"

"This depends on many factors," he said, holding her gaze. "Are you planning to return to Italy soon?"

Her forehead wrinkled, and she shook her head. "As of today, I'm on maternity leave."

Judging from her frown, she was not happy about this. Interesting. "You are free?"

"Apparently." She flashed him a tight smile. "My job is triggering higher blood pressure, so I am under doctor's orders to reduce my stress."

She gave him a pointed look those last words.

He studied her closer. "You have no plans for the next couple months except to take care of yourself and the baby, correct?"

"Correct," she said, then gave him a wary look. "Please don't follow that up with a marriage proposal."

Alessandro ignored the comment and gave her a seductive smile because a more specific plan was forming, one that gave him more time to introduce her to the pleasures he could provide for her. “I have a different proposal. Our family’s home sits in the foothills of the Alps, amid a countryside that guidebooks call charming. The temperature is warm and mild this time of year, and you can enjoy a swimming pool, fresh-baked pastries from the local bakery, naps and anything else that you may like.”

Her eyes widened with unmistakable interest. Yes, pleasure was the right path. She claimed she didn’t want his wealth *per se*, but just as he had thought, she would enjoy the spoils of it.

“And this enormous house just sits empty?” There was a hint of censure in her voice that he couldn’t read.

“It’s a country retreat. I assure you, it’s well kept.”

She tilted her head to the side, and her gaze was penetrating. “And you, of course, will be busy working.”

Alessandro could hear the edge in her voice. This was a test, and he was not sure she even knew what answer she wanted from him. But he had learned from her comment earlier when he had made the calculation error of letting her know she and the baby would be alone. This was not what she wanted.

For the last seven months he did not seek her out, despite the way his body ached for her, he reminded himself. He could remain under control. So he offered her a compromise. “I will stay there when I can get away, if that is what you want.”

“Italy is lovely this time of the year,” she said, almost to herself. Ann-Sophie, whose job was to be a neutral medium for others' ideas, looked so far from neutral right now. He let her debate this option as they ate. After a few moments of silence, she set down her fork and straightened in her chair.

"Thank you for the offer," she said carefully, "but I'm fine where I am."

But Alessandro had not brought his family's company and name back from ruin by laying all his cards on the table in the first round of negotiation. He hadn't even begun to use all the tools he could leverage. But for now, he focused on the lowest-hanging fruit: This woman loved books. She loved to read, as was clear from the half-read books scattered across her living room.

So he turned to her and smiled. "I neglected to mention a feature of this house that might be of particular interest. We have an enormous library. Perhaps you would at least like to see it?"

CHAPTER FOUR

Two weeks.

Ann-Sophie had given herself two weeks to negotiate how to handle co-parenting their baby. They had to come to an agreement somehow, and if it happened in a country retreat in the idyllic Italian hills, well, that qualified as the vacation Dr. Azzizi had recommended. As Alessandro steered his sleek sports car along the winding two-lane road, Ann-Sophie reminded herself that there was no reason to feel anxious. Yes, she had agreed to this plan in a moment of weakness—how could she resist a library?—but she was on holiday. And in between enjoying all the extravagant luxuries Alessandro had promised, she planned to uncover why he was so set on marriage.

They had landed on a private airstrip, surrounded by lush trees that still wore their summer greens, but now, as Alessandro's steered them toward the Alps, she spotted glimmers of fall. Golden grains from the fields of the lowlands had now made way for endless ribbons of grapevines that lined the foothills, their leaves flaunting hints of oranges and deep reds at the tips. The warm air that blew through the open windows of the red two-seater caressed her, lulling her into a kind of dreamy state, where questions about the future and Alessandro's role in it didn't weigh quite so heavily on her.

This morning, Alessandro had arrived in a well-cut suit, clean-shaven, his dark, glossy hair combed off his face, as if he was ready for a board meeting. The only word she had for the complicated mess of feelings that stirred at the sight of him was relief. Relief as his intoxicating gaze washed over her, and relief that she might not have to care for the baby entirely on her own. Ann-Sophie knew both those feelings were just that—*feelings*, fickle and fleeting, not more concrete realities.

She couldn't forget that he wanted more than just two weeks in Italy from her. He wanted marriage and would likely pursue this goal relentlessly. Alessandro had the kind of wealth that could make too much of the world fall at his feet. He had been raised to expect that he should be the master of his own destiny, so she knew better than to trust any fantasies about the future. The moment he changed his mind, the moment she was not expedient, he could set her to the side. Along with the baby. And she knew too well how much damage that could bring to a child.

Two weeks, she reminded herself. She could leave it anytime if everything became too much. It wasn't as if she would be some sort of captive in his castle, guarded with impenetrable walls and a crocodile-infested moat…would she?

Ann-Sophie turned to him. "The place you're taking me… This was your family's country escape?"

"Massimo and I lived here for a number of years, until we left for boarding school."

She wrinkled her brow at the wording of his answer. "With you parents, right?"

"Occasionally," he said, and there was a guarded note in his voice, as if she had stumbled into well-guarded territory. "My father had business in Milan, of course, and the two of us were a handful. One of the many perks of wealth is that you can hire staff for anything."

There was a twist of bitterness in his voice, but when she glanced over at him, he gave her one of his distracting smiles. It was unsettling how well it worked on her. Right now, with the warm breeze blowing through his hair and his sleeves rolled up, exposing his forearms as he gripped the steering wheel, Alessandro Carandini was more attractive than any man had the right to be.

But after the past day with him, she could see the way he used charm and distraction as tools to get what he wanted, and currently he wanted something from her. That awareness spread through her again, reminding her of just how vulnerable she was to him. Maybe it was better to address their relationship directly.

"I just wanted to be clear about this…" She gestured between the two of them. He glanced at her, one eyebrow lifted.

"We won't be…?" She hesitated.

"Yes?" There was a hint of amusement that teased at the corners of his lips, but he waited for her to explain what she was almost sure was perfectly obvious. Also, she was completely failing at being direct. Her face felt hot, and her blush was certainly obvious. Everything back in Nice had flowed so easily between them, and right now, when he was purposely making this conversation difficult for her, it was clear how easily he controlled the flow.

She let out a little huff of a breath. "I'm talking about the bedroom."

"Is that a proposition?" He looked in her direction and his eyes raked down her body. "I'm definitely open to it, though I usually like a woman to buy me a meal first."

The humor caught her by enough surprise that it cut through her embarrassment. And for a moment, she forgot the mess of her life and the uncertainty of their future and just laughed. After seven months of worries, it felt so good to let go and laugh. It felt dangerously like stepping back in time, to those nights before he so abruptly shut down any questions of future contact.

"I'll keep that in mind," she said. "But my question is about sleeping arrangements."

"I have alerted Olivia to prepare a room for you, though you are free to stay in my bed as often as you wish."

She flushed at a particularly clear memory of lying next to him in bed. "As long as I take you to supper first, of course."

"Of course," he said. Then his expression shifted into something more businesslike. "I have also arranged for a doctor to visit for checkups. In case you change your mind about the paternity test."

Frustration rose inside, still so close to the surface. "I haven't."

"Why not?" he asked softly.

She swallowed, fighting the urge to turn away. Instead, she forced herself to be direct.

"I know that I would not be sitting here in your car if I weren't carrying your child. But nothing between us—co-parenting, let alone marriage—will work if you can't trust me. And I need to know—" She stopped. Swallowed. She didn't need to reveal any more vulnerabilities at this point. "You're going to have to trust that there has been no one else."

His eyes darkened with a gleam at the words *no one else*, and if she didn't know better, she might have called it jealousy.

"Trust is something to be earned, *cara*. But I will let you decide, of course," he said smoothly, though she was almost sure they were not done with the subject.

Alessandro slowed the car at a fork and turned onto a narrow road, a path through a grove of olive trees that curved until she could make out a village. Huddles of whitewashed houses with terra-cotta roofs climbed the hillside, peeking out from behind one another as if they were watching for her arrival. Above them on the hill was what could only be described as a castle. Stark, sturdy towers rose up above steep stone walls, and she caught glimpses of the roofs of a sprawling set of buildings that this fortress protected.

Ann-Sophie did not need confirmation from Alessandro to understand that they were not headed for one of the quaint, whitewashed houses in town. He was a

Carandini. Of course, he was taking her to an actual castle, and, of course, he hadn't thought to mention this. In a twist she should have foreseen, she was, in fact, going to be living inside the walls of a fortress for the next two weeks. The possibility of a moat looked questionable in this sun-dried land, and she hoped the same for crocodiles lurking in its murky waters.

Alessandro raked a hand through his hair as he navigated through the narrow stone streets of the village. Here in this fancy sports car, against the backdrop of charming shops and blooming window boxes, he looked much more like the man she remembered and less like the polished businessman that had shown up on her doorstep. More at ease. They passed cafés, bakeries and a small square that held a church and other stately buildings. The town was built in a mix of stone and peeling coats of whitewash, which gave it a look of rustic elegance.

"Does this village have a hotel?" she asked.

Alessandro glanced at her, lifting a skeptical eyebrow. "Are you contemplating alternate accommodations?"

"Maybe." That sounded better than an escape route.

The line of houses came to an end, and they made their final ascent to his family's property. The entire wall of the fortress looked as if it had been built and rebuilt countless times. It was a mix of rough-hewn rock, bricks and finely chiseled stones—definitely solid. The only sign of a moat was a trickling creek that flowed under the narrow bridge just before the entrance. If crocodiles had ever walked this path, they had left long ago in search of swampier grounds.

An iron gate twisted and curled between the pillars that held it, and it swung open theatrically as they neared. Alessandro drove across the bridge, and they entered a cobblestone courtyard. Sprawled out in front of them in the same patchwork of stone was a rambling, castle-like villa. Stained-glass windows glittered from the majestic towers, and arched passages, covered with flowering vines, stretched across the lower levels. Before Ann-Sophie could take in any more details, Alessandro turned into a long, covered terrace, brought the car to a stop and turned off the engine. She blinked, trying to orient herself in this place. It felt as if she was dreaming, and she hadn't even seen the library yet.

Alessandro came around to her door to help her out, which saved her about five minutes of awkward struggle. When she stood up, her body so close to his, she felt the same thrill of awareness as she had the day before in her living room.

"Welcome to my family's retreat," he said, his voice low and rough, as if he was feeling the same hot current of desire. "I hope it meets your expectations."

Ann-Sophie drew in a breath, trying to focus on her surroundings and not on the man who stood so temptingly close. Though she had toured impressive castles all over the world, they had felt like museums, tied to an impersonal history. But this place was…alive. Almost magical. Somehow, despite knowing that the Carandini family moved in Italy's most elite circles, she wasn't prepared for a place like this. Maybe it was the word *retreat*, which brought to mind the cabin she and her mother had stayed in for a few summers. It had been smaller than the garage in front of her, and the only bath was a dip in the cold lake a short walk away. This walled estate was so laughably far from that.

She started along the cobblestone path, with Alessandro distractingly close by her side. When they reached the main courtyard, where a fountain gurgled, she realized why her mind had gone so incongruously to that tiny cabin in the Swedish countryside. This place was quiet in the same way, without the sounds of the city. Instead, it was alive with the twitters and squawks of birds and the rustle of leaves in the warm breeze. And though its gracefully sloping roof and arched entryway was so far from a cabin in Sweden, for a moment, she felt…at home. *Don't get comfortable*, she reminded herself. This was just for two weeks.

"How long has this place been in your family?" she asked as they walked along the well-worn stone path.

"My grandfather purchased it when the business grew. He was originally from this area and wanted to make sure our family's roots stayed here."

There was a way Alessandro talked about his family that she didn't understand, a distance, as if it wasn't his own family he was discussing but a general period of history he was recounting.

"Did your grandparents live here with you?" she asked.

"They gave the villa to my parents so they could raise their children," he said, and his tone was even more distant, despite the fact that these "children" included Alessandro. “My grandparents did everything they could to guide my father. This place for us, a position in the company, but in the end, he and my mother weren’t interested in any of it. My brother understood this much earlier, but I was the fool who defended them for years.”

His voice never wavered or showed any hint of emotion, but his words took Ann-Sophie’s breath away. She turned, studying the sharp cut of his jaw, the proud line of his forehead, looking for signs of emotion, but she saw no distress. She had no idea what to make of any of this.

They entered the villa through a heavy wooden door, and Ann-Sophie found herself in an extravagant hallway. The ceilings were lined with dark wood, each plank carved and polished, and the floors were tiled in the same terra-cotta as the roofs, covered with area rugs in lush reds and blues.

“All your needs will be taken care of by the household staff,” he said as they walked across the front entryway, toward an elegant staircase.

Household staff. Ann-Sophie resisted an eye roll, though she supposed she wouldn’t miss doing her own laundry. “I probably need to talk to someone about a low-salt diet.”

“I have given Olivia an overview of your situation and general precautions, but please let her know any specifics,” he said, and she couldn’t help but notice that his voice was no longer devoid of emotion. When he mentioned Olivia, she heard the kind of warmth he seemed to reserve for his brother. “She fed and kept track of two rambunctious boys. I guarantee nothing you request will pose anywhere near the challenge we did."

Alessandro led her up the staircase and to another hallway, lined with marble busts and paintings of sprawling landscapes in gilded frames. He stopped in front of a door near the end of the hall.

"You may have your choice of bedrooms, of course," he said in that lazy, sexy voice of his, and the word *bedrooms* sent a rush of awareness through her. "But I asked Olivia to prepare one I think you would particularly like."

He opened the door into a room decorated with the same dark, intricately carved woods as the hallway. Across the room, French doors led to a balcony, muted in the sunlight, and on the far side was a majestic bed covered in a silky red bedspread that looked like temptation incarnate. But all of this was eclipsed by shelf after shelf of books. Was she sleeping in the library?

"This is lovely," she said, her voice breathless.

"I'm pleased you like it, but there is another reason why I chose this one for you."

A smile teased at her lips. "Let me guess. Your bedroom is next door?"

"It is." He flashed his heart-stopping smile, so full of the humor she remembered. Her heart thumped harder. "But I suspect you might like what I'm about to show you even better."

Alessandro led her to a door along the sidewall, under an intricately carved wooden threshold. He turned the handle and revealed an area far too vast to be called a room, even in this castle-like place. As she walked out onto a stone balcony, she could see she was in one of the villa's towers she had spied from the road. At some point, the balconies that lined each level had likely been used for defense, but now the stone hallways were lined with wooden shelves, stacked with countless rows of books. Her room was just a teaser. This was the place Alessandro had used to lure her here, and it was even more spectacular than she had imagined.

Ann-Sophie walked to the edge of the balcony and rested her hands on the polished stone, gazing down the open center. Lit in the rosy golden light of the stained-glass windows was a spiral staircase in the same dark wood as the shelves, and at the corners of each level were small alcoves, fitted with armchairs and lamps, like tiny reading rooms.

Alessandro rested his hand on the curve of her back, and a new feeling rushed through her, one she refused to call hope. He leaned closer and whispered in her ear, "Welcome to the Carandini family library."

She had given him two weeks, and that was exactly what he needed. He would ease her defenses down and seduce her in every way possible again. Marry her. And the restless feeling she stirred in him? The risk of exposing the raw edge this villa evoked in him, haunted by the ghosts of his own past? Anything could be managed for two weeks. Of course, he would let himself indulge in pleasures. Those alone weren't a risk. It was allowing these pleasures and indulgences to take over his emotions.

Which were absolutely under control now.

The more he had gotten used to the idea of this pregnancy, the more he saw the opportunity it presented. A baby of his own would mean a chance to right the wrongs of his childhood. He would never deceive his child. He could never shower this child with false affection, then cast them away when they became an inconvenience with a sprinkle of half-hearted gaslighting. He would set clear expectations and follow through, not blame a child for things they were too young to understand.

"I can't believe your family owns all of this," said Ann-Sophie softly, as she gestured at the shelves.

"It's an impressive collection," he agreed.

"Just looking at all these books makes me outrageously happy," said Ann-Sophie, shaking her head.

The tension that he had carried in his shoulders since the moment his brother had told him about her *roundness* was finally starting to ease. If she could be coaxed into raising the child here at the estate, with its library and the walls, this would contain the unpredictability of their…situation. So Alessandro took a deep breath and let himself enjoy the soft material of her dress under his hand and the lavender scent of her hair.

"This was my great-aunt's life's work," he said, watching Ann-Sophie's features, studying her reactions. "In another era, from another family, she likely would have been an academic. But she and my grandfather grew up without means, and she could never get her hands on enough books. So when my grandfather's fortune exceeded anyone's dreams, he gave this project to her."

"Am I staying in her room?"

"When she stayed here, yes. Though she chose to live in the home where she and my grandfather grew up, she spent a good amount of time here, building the library of her dreams."

"Interesting," she said, but creases were forming on her forehead. She looked up at him, her eyes wide and unguarded. "All of these books just *sit here* in this house, where no one lives?"

She sounded…displeased by that idea. He frowned. "Not anymore. You are here to read them."

She tilted her head a little, as if to consider his answer. After a moment, she said, "Show me around."

Alessandro gestured to the main floor below, where a series of cases stood at the center. "The oldest books are shelved on the bottom floor, away from direct sunlight, where the room temperature can be more carefully controlled."

She nodded, then began to wander along the balcony, taking in the rows of books that glowed in the red light of the stained glass. Alessandro found himself entranced by the way her hair glittered and moved as she reached for one volume, then another.

"The remaining floors of stacks are for more recent books, arranged by language, I believe. You might find something in Swedish."

Ann-Sophie continued slowly, her gaze fixed on the

shelves as they passed. She stopped, stooped down and then rose. "Did you grandparents love to read, too?"

"Like many people with new money, my grandfather likely saw this project more as an opportunity to establish the family's prestige."

She frowned a little, and Alessandro found a strange twinge of…displeasure. As if he had wanted her approval. But that couldn't be right. He focused on the fact that her voice had lost the bite he had heard in Stockholm, and right now, she looked like she had in Nice, so curious, so unselfconscious. Except that she was, indeed, rounder. Gloriously so.

His family was not a topic he volunteered information about, as the conversation could so easily slide into territory better left in the past. But this past would soon be part of his child's history, too. The idea had stirred something inside him, unfamiliar and uncomfortable.

"Where did all of these books come from?" she asked.

"Some were here when my grandparents bought the place, which was how the project started. The rest came from auctions, estate sales, travel…everywhere. My great-aunt developed a bit of a reputation, so libraries came to her with older books in need of costly restoration or books they no longer had room for."

"This place definitely has the space," she said, and he heard a trace of awe in her voice.

"If there is anything you want to add to the collection, please let me know."

She shook her head slowly, as if she couldn't quite believe what was in front of her. She continued to wander until she came to an alcove with a velvet armchair and a small table with a reading lamp. "I think I'd start with more readers."

He blinked at her, then nodded. "I'm sure that can be accommodated."

Ann-Sophie let her hand brush over the soft velvet of the armchair that sat in the rays of the afternoon sun.

"My aunt built these nooks on each floor to make sure she could find natural light for reading, no matter the season or time of day."

Ann-Sophie turned to him. "Do you have a favorite place to read?"

"Not much of a reader. Never have been." The moment he said this, her expression fell. She looked… disappointed in him, and he found himself very displeased by this. Displeased enough to reveal a truth he so rarely spoke of, before he could think better of it. "Dyslexia."

"Oh," she whispered, and the hint of judgment that he had seen on her face shifted to something softer.

Alessandro was well aware that this was exactly the kind of softening he needed to exploit. The plan was to use this…emotional reaction he was having to the unearthing of his past, he reminded himself. His most strategic move was to show her a glimpse of what she wanted to see, then shut it all down again.

"My parents preferred the term *lazy*," he added, forcing himself to reveal his past. "My father was particularly affronted by the idea that there was something 'wrong' with his son—his words."

"I'm so sorry," Ann-Sophie whispered. "That's awful."

Her blue eyes seemed to pierce through all his protective layers, leaving him with the disquieting sense that she was *seeing* him.

Alessandro waved off her sympathy. "By that point, it probably didn't matter. I had already decided that being spectacularly bad was much better than being the kid who always needed extra help."

She furrowed her brow. "But they still should have—"

"We don't need to adjudicate my childhood," he snapped. "I've moved on."

Ann-Sophie blinked at the sharpness in his voice. "I'm sorry for prying."

But her penetrating gaze stayed fixed on him, as if she was seeing even more. He felt…off balance.

Warning bells clanged in his head, reminding him of the last time this happened, when he lashed out at her back in Nice. He would absolutely not lash out at her, but he had to do *something*. So he did the only other thing that he could think of. It was the thing that he had needed to do since the moment she had walked down her own street and back into his life. Slowly, so there was no mistaking what his intentions were, he lowered his mouth so it was almost touching hers. She blinked up at him, her eyes widening in surprise. And then he saw the shift, the look he had not allowed himself to imagine for seven months. Open desire, just for him. But now that she was so inescapably close, right in front of him, he stopped resisting.

He closed the distance and gave in. Her lips were as soft as he remembered, and they tasted of that sweet, forbidden fruit he had kept from himself for far too long. His body reacted to the taste immediately with electric arousal. This was the heaven he had been waiting for. He brushed his mouth against hers again, telling himself that this was part of his plan.

He wanted more, so he opened his lips to hers. Her breath hitched, and a wave of satisfaction ran through him. Yes, she wanted him, and he could have her again. The thought echoed inside him, stronger than he expected, the moment she parted her lips. Her soft mouth was hungry, and he could taste a want that matched his own. The fire that had burned unbearably high every night of that one, glorious week flared higher.

Alessandro cradled her jaw in his hands, aching for more of the eager strokes of her soft tongue. He ran his hands over her shoulders and down her arms, remembering each dip and swell. Then he found her waist, testing the changes that he had seen with his eyes. But the touch was so much better. Slowly, he moved his hands over her new roundness, caressing—

He felt movement under his hand. Their child, so undeniably real. Something strong and painful rip-roared through him, turning the heat that moved through him into ice. It was as if a long-healed wound had been forced open, and he needed to staunch the flow of fear and dread.

Alessandro pulled back and looked down at his hands, frozen on each side of her belly. He glanced up at Ann-Sophie, at the crease that had formed between her eyebrows, her unspoken questions hanging between them. He refused to answer them. Instead, he backed away and removed his hands. His body protested loudly, and he clenched his fists, resisting the urge to reach for her. He took a step away. Her eyes were wide, and her hair tousled. Her cheeks had flushed, and the confusion written across her face was mixed with raw want.

Then her mouth twisted down with what could have been hurt. Alessandro clenched his hands to stop himself from reaching for her again, from touching her, from doing so much more than kissing her, just to soothe that hurt away. But he would not subject himself to the emotions that still tore at him. So he took one more step back, ignoring the twist in his gut as Ann-Sophie's expression grew more guarded.

And when he spoke, his voice was fully under control. "Supper is served out in the garden at seven."

Then he turned and walked away.

CHAPTER FIVE

Ann-Sophie stood, frozen in place, as Alessandro's last footsteps echoed on the stone walkway of the tower. When the door closed behind him, she sank into the lush velvet chair, her mind reeling. Was he just…walking away? After that kiss?

For one, short moment it had felt as though Alessandro had exposed a guarded piece of himself, and then they were kissing with a magic that entwined this enchanting library with the man she had lost herself with seven months ago. Seven months of longing came alive, longing she had tried to repress. His lips had caressed hers with the same aching hunger she remembered too well.

And then, just as unexpectedly as this magical moment had started, Alessandro took it away, leaving her with this sensation that something in her was cracking as he walked away. And she was doing all she could to hold herself together.

Maybe she should have foreseen this possibility… and prepared for it. But Ann-Sophie had spent years telling herself and everyone around her that she couldn't be abandoned by a father who had never been there in the first place. Now, she was suddenly faced with the fact that she was absolutely not Just Fine, Thank You, despite the countless times she had said it. Because the moment she pictured the way Alessandro had stared at her belly as the baby kicked, his expression a mask of horror, she knew where this was going.

He was going to leave them.

This made no sense when she considered his expressed desire to marry her, and yet she had felt his reaction viscerally. It had been a live wire straight to the place where she had buried her grief. He had found that place, and her instinct was to flee, to go back to Stockholm. She told herself she could. But first, they needed to come to some sort of agreement about the child, even if it didn't involve the marriage he demanded.

Ann-Sophie had no idea what to do with all these thoughts. The sun filtered through the windows, casting long rays of light across the tower and lighting up the place. She wanted to disappear in this quiet tower library for a while and try to settle her thoughts. Also, at the moment, she was stuck in the chair and too exhausted to get herself out of it. She was so very tired, and this seemed to be the perfect place to take a nap. Then again, everywhere seemed to be the perfect place to take a nap these days, so Ann-Sophie propped her feet on the matching red velvet footstool and let herself drift off to sleep.

She had no idea how long she slept, but when she opened her eyes again, the light had completely changed in the glow of the evening. Also, her stomach was like an empty, clawing pit of hunger. She hadn't eaten since the plane ride, and she was thirsty enough to drink the moat water. Ann-Sophie wrestled with the chair and managed to get herself to standing. She walked through the quiet halls, tracing her way back to the courtyard, then began to circle the house looking for Alessandro. When she found him, they would have a talk about the way he turned on her so suddenly. A bit of food would hopefully help her get her thoughts in order.

She walked through vine-covered archways and past a pool tiled in blues and whites until she came to a terrace with a table, shaded by a large umbrella. The terrace was covered in tiles in the same terracotta with accents painted in bright blues and whites in a pattern along the low walls that surrounded it. Just beyond, the breathtaking countryside spread out in front of her, dotted with orchards and vineyards. The table was covered with a white tablecloth, and on top of it, she spotted a pitcher of water. Relief rushed through her as she crossed the patio, grabbed a large glass and poured it full of water. She drank it in a few short gulps, but as she set it down, she took in what she had missed in her desperate thirst: Only one place on the table was set. She blinked, frowning. Were she and Alessandro eating separately?

A door creaked behind her, then footsteps, and her traitorous heart beat harder. She turned, but it was not Alessandro. It was a woman with brown hair streaked with gray, and she was carrying a tray of food. The woman smiled at her in such a motherly way, but after

Alessandro's comments, Ann-Sophie knew that this was not his mother.

"I am Olivia," she said, setting a bowl of soup in front of her on the table, followed by a small cutting board with a loaf of fresh baked bread and olive oil. "Welcome to Villa Carandini."

"I'm Ann-Sophie, Alessandro's..." She had no words in Italian—or in her native Swedish—to neatly describe what they were. Then again, her unwieldy stomach spoke for itself.

Olivia's smile grew. "Alessandro told me about you. Please, be seated. He left me with instructions to make sure you are well fed and cared for."

Her mind immediately focused on the word *left*. "Alessandro is not here?"

Olivia shook her head sympathetically. "He had urgent business in Milan. But I am here to take care of everything you need."

Not quite everything, she thought darkly, but she smiled and thanked Olivia, wondering just how much the woman understood of their situation.

"I'll return with your second course when you are ready," said Olivia and she disappeared inside the villa. Ann-Sophie ate a spoonful of delicate tomato bisque, trying to get her mind around the fact that Alessandro had not only walked away from her, but also felt the need to use his car to put distance between them. With the flimsiest of excuses, no less. Where was the trust he spoke of so pointedly back in Stockholm? Ann-Sophie looked around at the castle-like place that rose up around her and the swimming pool that shimmered in the evening lights. All this beauty did nothing to ease the sinking sensation inside her.

Just as she had thought. Alessandro had abandoned her.

This event should be enough to rule out completely the idea of a marriage. She would never let her child be raised by a father who would leave them. Ann-Sophie cut herself a thick slab of bread and dipped it in the olive oil, so rich and lemony it brought tears to her eyes. Or maybe the tears were about something else. But she would *not* cry over this man. She swallowed and looked out at the last rays of sun that glittered across the valley until she felt a little less emotional. When the warm evening breeze worked its magic, she tried to look at the situation more rationally. Alessandro's abrupt change in mood suggested he'd been rattled by their kiss, and for the first time she wondered if he was just as overwhelmed by their situation as she was.

Olivia appeared moments later with a heaping plate of pasta with roasted vegetables and prosciutto. Before she could walk away, Ann-Sophie asked, "Do you have a moment?"

"Of course," said the woman and sat down in the chair next to her.

She had so many questions about Alessandro, but asking them would show how little she knew about the man whom she was having a child with. Or maybe it was too late to care about that.

"How long have you known Alessandro?"

Olivia smiled. "My sister and I were hired to care for the boys from the moment that Alessandro and Massimo were old enough to walk and get into trouble. And they were definitely trouble."

Ann-Sophie tried to imagine Alessandro and his brother as little boys getting into mischief. How did a playful boy turn into the man who had so coldly walked away from her?

"Their parents must have appreciated your work," she said carefully. Nannies were de rigueur in upper-class households, and yet from Alessandro's comments, she suspected that this arrangement was more complicated.

"Their grandmother hired us," said Olivia, and there was a protectiveness in her voice. Alessandro had hinted at a carelessness in his parents' relationship with them when they had driven in the car that Olivia's answer seemed to confirm.

Ann-Sophie felt an uncomfortable twist of sympathy in her stomach, despite her frustrations. She herself had had a father who had no interest in her, and despite the fact that she had been surrounded by her mother, her grandparents and so many aunts, both those by blood and those by choice, it didn't take away that sorrow of a parent who did not care. Ann-Sophie looked around at the decadent wealth of Alessandro's childhood. More money and more luxuries would not have fixed any of the weight of her hurt, and she imagined it was the same for him.

"How often does Alessandro visit now?" she asked.

"He and his brother celebrate holidays here."

"Does he bring dates?" She bit her lip, wishing she could take her question back.

Olivia paused, giving her a searching luck. "He could. But he never has. Ever."

Until this unexpected pregnancy.

"I can't imagine owning this whole place and leaving it empty," she said.

"It's hardly empty," said Olivia with a laugh. "My family lives here."

Ann-Sophie's face heated. "Sorry."

Olivia waved off her apology, and her expression turned more serious. "When the twins' grandfather bought this villa, the surrounding wall was crumbling, threatening our town. The old owner didn't have the money to fix it, and the state wasn't going to take on the project. Everyone in the village was grateful the Carandinis did. If the family had not bought that property, half of the village's houses would likely be rubble at this point. One of the winter rains would have certainly swept away the wall, taking with it the whole village. Before they came, some breach of the wall took out a few houses on the hillside below. So in the eyes of the town they are welcome to come and go as they please as long as they continue to maintain the place. And both Massimo and Alessandro have promised that."

How nice that Olivia found Alessandro reliable. Trustworthy. Pretty much the opposite of her experience.

"Ah, it's my brother, who is supposed to be at the villa negotiating a marriage that won't singlehandedly destroy our family's reputation we have worked so hard to fix," said Massimo as he leaned against the door to his office, his hands in his pockets, his intense gaze unrelenting. His tone was deceptively casual, but Alessandro could hear the bite in his brother's subtle rebuke. Alessandro had never cared much about his own reputation, but both his grandfather and Massimo had dedicated their lives to the family name. He had spent his teens making both their lives more difficult, and he had sworn he would not do that again. Now, Massimo was invoking the family name, what all their work was supposed to be for.

"Are you back in the office to announce the date of your nuptials?"

"I will take care of it in the next couple weeks," grumbled Alessandro.

He kept his eyes on the screen in front of him, though he had no illusions that Massimo would believe he was reading. The truth was that he had spent the entire morning staring at the same pages. Going word by word through a document had always taken a great deal of concentration, and today it seemed impossible. In truth, he had never spent much time exploring adaptations that could have helped. Maybe the label of laziness was not so far from the mark. Both his parents treated that label with indifference, which Alessandro found far less painful than the scorn they reserved for a learning disability. Looking back, Alessandro wouldn't have called any of his choices during his teens conscious ones. They had been more intuition, which had been his saving grace for so much of his life. Until now.

"Catarina and I would like to attend your wedding.

In addition to my hopes that you will also find a path to love…" His brother paused, as if he was thinking of his own surprising path. "I want to head off any speculation that this marriage is a last-minute decision so the child is not born out of wedlock."

Alessandro met his brother's gaze. "It is a last-minute decision so the child is not born out of wedlock. For the family."

This truth was so much easier to speak than the turmoil of emotions that had exploded inside him the moment he had felt a tiny kick from inside Ann-Sophie's stomach. It was no secret that he and Massimo had both dedicated their adult lives to rebuilding the company *for the family.* Just one generation ago, his parents' volatile, explosive relationship had bankrupted the family business and ruined every ounce of good will that his grandfather had carefully built up for his entire career. His parents' relationship had consumed them, so caught in indulgence and petty jealousies and social one-upmanships that it didn't leave time for anything as mundane as running a business. Let alone raising two boys.

The previous year, when Massimo's and Alessandro's acumen, strategy and dedication to their business had still not been enough to quell the speculation that the brothers would get distracted by the kind of relationship that had sunk the Carandini family's reputation and fortune, Massimo had arranged a marriage for the explicit purpose of extinguishing these worries. The plan had worked, both as a public-relations campaign and also privately, to the unexpected satisfaction of his brother. That was supposed to be the end of it.

Now, Alessandro's unanticipated baby threatened the balance that Massimo had gained for the family. Alessandro had made sure he was held to a different standard, that affairs should be expected and would not affect any other part of his life. But, as his brother had rightly pointed out, people would tolerate that behavior only so far.

When Massimo didn't respond, he added, "This is not the direction I saw for my life."

As the words came out of his mouth, the image of Ann-Sophie on his bed that had come to him in Nice reappeared in his mind. He had, in fact, imagined this life, and that image had filled him with an emotion too volatile to handle. "But I will not allow another generation to be brought up the way we were. I will be there for my child."

"I understand," said his brother, his voice softer. "I also want to show that the family is behind you."

Alessandro gave Massimo a nod of gratitude. His brother would always be behind him, even if they didn't always understand each other.

"Your well-known charm is noticeably absent," added Massimo, raising an eyebrow. "This is the one time all those years of practice should be used."

Alessandro could have answered with a flippant comment and moved on, but he didn't. Instead, he tried to put into words something he had been stewing on all day.

"Some part of me just shuts down." He frowned and added, "I learned to be charming for a reason."

Even saying those words were painful. They brought him back to a time when his selfish anger had controlled him.

His brother frowned. "You are not the same man you were then."

"I am not the same man because I have kept all these impulses in check. I don't think I'm capable of anything that looks like what a family should." The emotions he had felt when he and Ann-Sophie kissed had been so full of the hurt he had built himself up from all those years ago. "Our parents were not suited to have children, and neither am I."

His brother looked like he had plenty more to say on that subject, but he just shook his head. "Save that problem for after the wedding. Right now, you need to get this woman to the altar before she has a baby out of wedlock."

"For the family," Alessandro added with a humorless smile.

"Go back, and I will cover you for the next two weeks," said his brother. "Keep me updated about the wedding."

He couldn't bring himself to resent Massimo's focus on the wedding *for the family*—a plan that Alessandro himself had come up with back in Stockholm. Maybe it was the universe's idea of payback, since he had pushed his own brother into a marriage to a person he had never met? At least Alessandro had chosen his partner himself. And they were undeniably well-suited in the bedroom. Too well-suited, he thought darkly.

As Alessandro left the city behind and drove into the countryside, the rolling hills of his childhood spreading out on either side, Massimo's advice ran through his head: Focus on the wedding, and deal with the rest later. It was questions concerning the future that provoked the eruption of his long-controlled feelings. Until he had secured her agreement, he would block these thoughts from his mind.

Alessandro turned off the main road, through the olive grove, and entered the little village that had been his home for the first years of his life. It had been a long time since he had spent time here, and he made a mental note to ask Olivia about the best bakeries, the most charming areas to show to Ann-Sophie. Would she agree to raise their child here? By the time he climbed the staircase and walked the long, familiar hall, he felt more like himself than he had in the last two days. Anything that was uncertain, he would put off until after the marriage.

Long ago, he and Massimo had learned the lesson that though people told themselves they made important decisions with logic, it so often wasn't true. They made decisions with their hearts. This was why he had earned the rightful place as the silver-tongued charmer. Because for all the pain his parents' emotional manipulations and nastiness had caused him, they had given him skills that he had sharpened into a tool that was just as useful as Massimo's strategic planning. Alessandro could sway people's emotions. He would lead

Ann-Sophie to the inescapable conclusion that marriage was the solution that her heart wanted, and he would enjoy the pleasures that this would entail.

But as he came to a stop in front of her doorway, Alessandro felt a twist in his gut. Was it guilt? It couldn't be, not for showering his future wife with attention. This was nothing like the games his parents played with each other. Any misconceptions she might develop were issues for after marriage, and he was not going to consider them before their wedding. So he pushed away the discomfort, telling himself he would only listen to that feeling the moment he walked out of the church with rings on their fingers.

Then he turned the knob to the door of her room and walked in.

Ann-Sophie sat in an antique armchair next to the open French doors, and the warm, sweet breeze blew through her sun-drenched hair, making it shimmer in the light. She looked out the window as she sipped from an espresso cup, suggesting she hadn't heard him open the door. He took a moment to study her. She wore the pajamas he had asked Olivia to find in town and lay out for her, and the silky material spilled over her lush, round body, giving him tempting hints of her new curves. On the table next to her was a tray of breakfast choices. In addition to the fresh pastries and fruit, he spotted the *filmjölk* and granola she had kept in her kitchen, which he had sent his assistant to gather before they left Stockholm. Despite the late morning hour, she appeared to have awoken not so long before, as her cheeks were still flushed from sleep. Seeing her like this, enjoying a slow, indulgent morning, sent a surge of satisfaction through him.

He wanted to just watch her for a bit, search this peaceful scene for more clues about the woman he found so fascinating. He could admit this fascination to himself because it would act as fuel for the next two weeks of negotiations. But after another moment, he was not satisfied with just looking. He started across the room, and after a few steps, she turned, startled. She must have been expecting Olivia because her expression changed. Her eyes widened with surprise, then flashed with what he could have sworn was happiness before she schooled her features into something more guarded.

"I apologize for my absence," he said, his voice low and graveled. "It was unavoidable, but I returned as quickly as I could."

She wanted to believe that his absence was "unavoidable." She wanted to believe him because everything would be so much easier if he had left because of some sort of emergency, some event that would likely never happen again. Because then she could relax into this life that he was spreading in front of her. She could let herself imagine everything that she wanted it to be.

Right now, Alessandro was looking at her the way he had in Nice, his eyes no longer guarded, the distance she had felt suddenly gone. He was looking at her again like there was no place on earth that he would rather be than right there with her. Ann-Sophie's heart soared in her chest, and, oh, how she wanted all of this to be real. How she wanted to forget the way he had turned on her so quickly after the startling kiss in the library. Maybe she could have even put that aside if he hadn't done the same thing back in Nice, so easily shutting her out of his life.

Now, he reappeared, as if he could slip in and out of her life when the whim struck him?

"How kind of you to return so quickly," she said, letting a sharp bite leak into her voice. Ann-Sophie turned back to her coffee and took a sip, welcoming the familiar, bitter taste.

Alessandro moved closer, and when she didn't look up, he kneeled in front of her. He was so inescapably *there*. She had nowhere else to look except the hard line of his jaw and the shadows under his eyes. Ann-Sophie fought against the memory of the last time he was this close, in the library, when he kissed her with a magic that made her forget everything else.

"It was unavoidable," he repeated, and the word grated on her nerves. Then he flashed her an indulgent smile. Did he think he could use her attraction to wave away her disappearance? The nerve of this man…

"You left yesterday without warning," she snapped. "You said nothing about leaving to me."

Alessandro managed to look a little contrite. "I apologize. It won't happen again."

He raised his eyebrows, as if he was waiting patiently for her to calm down. As if he was *indulging* her. Which only provoked her further.

"My father left, and he didn't come back." The words exploded out of her. "I will not be blindsided by you."

Alessandro blinked, clearly unprepared for this burst of emotion. The last of his smile slid off his face. The room was silent, as if everything that surrounded her—the elegant furniture, the books, the extravagant paintings—was just as stunned that she had spoken these words as Ann-Sophie was.

"I'm sorry," he finally said. "I didn't know that."

"Disappearing is not okay for anyone," she said, biting out the words. "I shouldn't have to drag out my own baggage to make this point."

"You're right." His voice was soft, conciliatory.

He reached for her hand, but she pulled away. If he touched her right now, the frustration bubbling inside might turn into something rawer. But now that she had revealed this piece of her past, she found that she wasn't ready to stop.

"I've never met my father," she said, and her voice trembled a little. "He and my mother were assigned to the same team in Sri Lanka—he, a photographer and she, a journalist—and from then on, they often traveled together. They both loved the nomadic life of being on an international correspondence team and were passionate about making the world a better place through their work. They partnered so closely, so it was no surprise that their professional relationship drifted into something more."

Ann-Sophie had known this story since she was a teenager, and yet she had never spoken aloud. Now, a strange feeling swept through her, as if she was a child again, her mother's warnings of why she should never contact her father ringing in her head. She clung to every thread of anger because she would absolutely never cry over a man who couldn't bother with her.

"My mother told him that she was pregnant and wanted to keep the baby. She had always wanted a child and this was their opportunity. She told my father she loved him and that they could have a family together, working and traveling." Ann-Sophie fought to keep the armor of her anger up as she approached this next part. "He told her that he loved her, too, but he had no interest in a baby. He wanted nothing to do with the work of bringing up a child, nor did he want to drag a child along on assignments or take turns staying back. Basically, he gave her an ultimatum—him or the baby. And she chose me."

Her voice wavered a little at these last words. Her mother had been forced to start over, to find a new team to work with rather than face this painful choice every day. She gave up a man she was in love with because Ann-Sophie came along. This was the sacrifice that Ann-Sophie could never forget.

She already felt so vulnerable with Alessandro, who could so easily brush off sudden disappearances. If he was incapable of understanding her position, then no amount of negotiations would make a marriage viable. Now, with that baby coming so soon between them and the trigger of his leaving such a direct hit, that raw feeling scraped inside her.

"We both have been thrown into this situation, but abandonment is not acceptable for me or for my child. My mother made that decision for me, that an uninterested father was worse for a child than no father at all. She did not want me to have to face that pain as a child, and I am grateful for it. The way you just…" She struggled for the words for what had triggered this earthquake inside her, one she was still feeling the aftershocks of. "The way you shut out whatever this is between us—that can't happen. You can decide on your relationship with the baby, and I can't control that decision. But if you want marriage, you should know that this is a nonstarter for me."

"*Our* baby." He was looking at her with a seriousness that she hadn't seen before. He didn't speak again for a long time, and when he did, his voice was low and grave. "First, I will never abandon a child of mine. Ever. On this, I swear on everything that I love."

And she heard a deep resonance of truth in his voice, something that broke through her anger.

"Your parents weren't there for you," she whispered, almost to herself.

But he heard her, and he didn't look away. He lifted his hand to her cheek and stroked it with a gentleness that took her breath away. "I will not disappear without telling you again."

Despite all the reasons she should be wary of this declaration, something inside her eased. The loosening started in her belly and spread through her body, strong, and unexpected, and the heat that had been anger just moments ago turned into something else.

"I am truly sorry," he said, softly.

She brought her hand to his, tracing his long fingers, his warm hand, the cords of his muscular forearms, until she reached the rolled cuffs of his elegant shirt.

Oh, how she had missed him. Ann-Sophie had spent the last seven months trying so hard not to think about this simple truth, letting anger and indignation fill all the spaces where want might settle. Now, every feeling she had suppressed was crashing through her, so much more complicated than desire.

Or maybe this didn't have to be more complicated than desire. Maybe she could just…give in. Give herself a place for all the tension of the past days. Just a little bit.

His fingers traveled down her cheek, over the tender skin of her neck. He traced her collarbone, his fingers lingering just inside the opening of her silk top. The soft material of her pajamas brushed over her skin, and her breasts felt heavy and full as his gaze swept across her face, dipping down to her lips. When his eyes met hers again, they were lit with something that felt raw. Real. There was so much she didn't know about him, so much they had to work out, but right now, as he looked into her eyes, she felt their connection growing stronger. Attraction sparked and sizzled between them, but there was something else there, a contradiction, both an opening and a closing she didn't understand. *I am having a baby with this man.* The idea settled inside her with a flutter of happiness she wanted so badly to trust.

His lips were close. She knew the brush of those lips, the way it felt to have them on her neck, her breasts, everywhere, and her entire body ached for all of it. Silently, Alessandro offered her his hands. She took them, and when he helped her to standing, she brought her hands to his arms, feeling the hard muscles under his perfectly tailored shirt, remembering them. She continued her exploration, tracing the strength of his broad shoulders. Then she slid her hands into his silken black hair and urged him closer. He let out a low groan, a sound somewhere between desire and relief, and his hard mouth met hers. Finally, they were kissing again. She opened for him, and his tongue teased hers, but he slowed, kissing her with an aching tenderness that left her gasping for breath. She let her hands travel down his chest, memorizing, reminding herself of every inch of him. *This was real.*

His hands brushed over her body, and she tensed. She held her breath, waiting for his reaction, as his hands moved slowly over her stomach, exploring the round fullness. He groaned in that deep, masculine way that left no doubt that he was enjoying every moment of his exploration. She looked up at his eyes, heavy-lidded with pleasure. His thick lashes only partially shielded the heat that radiated from them.

"Many good marriages have been built on less than we have between us," he said, his voice rough.

A shimmer of wariness radiated through the languid haze of their kiss. "I suppose it depends on how one defines a good marriage."

"Marriage is whatever we would like it to be."

Of course, Alessandro Carandini thought about marriage as something that was up to him. Of course, a man of his wealth and power thought that what he wanted out of marriage was stronger than an institution that had survived for millennia. She supposed there was some truth to this idea, that everyone could negotiate their own path to some degree. And yet, if he was so bent on getting married, then there must be something inherent about it that he wanted. Maybe he was withholding that from her, or maybe he was only starting to figure this out. After all, she hadn't been prepared for the force of her own reaction. Either way, she would not simply trust that everything would turn out to her satisfaction simply because he said it would. Because, as he had so rightly pointed out, trust went both ways.

He was watching her in that way he had more than once since he had shown up at her door, as if he was making an assessment. Then he smiled. "I hope breakfast was to your satisfaction."

"Somehow it included my favorites from Sweden." She was still a little befuddled about how Olivia had managed this. But when his smile turned a little smug, she understood that he had been in charge of this feat. Back when he had taken stock of her refrigerator, he must have noted what she liked.

"I want to make sure that you are completely satisfied with your stay here," he said, that lazy smile teasing at his lips.

She had no idea what to do with this stunning, sexy, charming man in front of her, or with the overwhelming reactions she had to him. So she laughed. The Alessandro she had spent a week with was definitely back. And she was going to end up in bed with him very soon if she was standing this close to him much longer. Ann-Sophie had not ruled out that possibility, but she definitely needed to think it through under less… compelling circumstances.

"I would definitely be satisfied with a swim this morning," she said. In the pool, they would be outside within sight of others. Also, a little time without carrying the weight of the baby would be heavenly.

"In the bureau you will find a selection of suits in case that might be helpful." He leaned forward and brushed his lips against her cheek. "I look forward to seeing you there."

Alessandro dove into the pool and took a long, slow breaststroke under the surface, then another, letting the refreshingly cool water ease his body. When he reached the shallow end, he turned and sprinted at a punishing speed back toward the deep end. He continued back and forth across the pool, letting the temperature and the exercise soothe his body and his mind. Their kiss had fully awakened the desire that he had felt in Nice, but it was tangled with something new. He knew not to think too much about whatever that new thing was. His disappearance had almost ruined the plan for marriage—he had seen it in her face when she spoke of her father. Ann-Sophie had mentioned her father in passing during their week together, something about him being out of her life, but Alessandro had not registered the way that this had seemed shaped her until he had stumbled on her breaking point. He would not make that mistake again.

He pushed himself, lap after lap across the pool, until his thoughts dissolved, and there was only the cool water around him, shimmering in the sun. He stopped in the middle and stood, slicking back his hair. His control was restored.

Ann-Sophie was sitting at the edge of the shallow end. Her feet dangled in the water, and she leaned back, resting on her hands. Her lush belly was covered with a red swimsuit, a beacon that both called to him and warned him off.

"You didn't like the swimsuits Olivia provided?" he asked.

Ann-Sophie gave him one of her amused smiles. "I prefer the one I brought. I think the days of string bikinis have long passed for me."

"I beg to disagree." He knew better than to approach her right now. If he did, he wouldn't be able to stop himself from touching all her new curves, which he found himself thinking about more and more. Instead, he dove back under the water, cooling himself again, and came up in the deep end. "Will you join me?"

She shrugged. "I was going to, but all your lap swimming is exhausting just to watch."

"I'll pretend to drown for a few minutes if that helps," he said.

"No thank you. Then I'll feel obligated to save you, and I'm not sure I'm spritely enough to manage that." A gust of wind blew her hair across her face, and she tucked it behind her ear.

He flashed her a smile. "Another option is to splash you a few times."

"Fine. I'm getting in." She let out a sweet little huff, then slipped into the water and swam toward him, smiling. The relief of the cool water was written all over her face. He felt a surge of satisfaction that he had given this to her, a feeling that he refused to look too closely at.

"In the water, I feel a little bit more like my old self," she said.

"I like you the way you are," he said with a smirk.

She raised an eyebrow, as if she was matching these words against his reaction to her in the library.

"I can demonstrate how I feel," he said, and she laughed.

He was telling the truth. The explanation for his reaction was too complicated to get into. That would come later, after their marriage. Then he would deal with the part of him that had simply lost the ability to be the person he should be. But if he was going to make it through these next two weeks, he needed to focus on these moments, right now.

CHAPTER SIX

As one day drifted into the next, Ann-Sophie was lulled into a cocoon of the luxurious present. She could choose the quiet stillness of her favorite library alcove, bathed in sunlight, or she could chat with Olivia and her niece, Cinzia, as they washed and chopped the vast bounties of the day's harvest from the garden. But most of the time, she and Alessandro were together. They spent days at the pool, or walking through the groves of orange trees that were ripening in the countryside just outside the village. She ate fresh oranges from the trees with peels so soft they fell apart, and the sweet juice ran through her hands. Everything about her life right now could be summed up with the word *decadent*.

But there was one way that she had not yet given in to decadence. Every night, after a long, lingering supper on the terrace, filled with wandering conversation and course after course of freshly prepared foods, Alessandro would walk her to her room and kiss her with a hunger he didn't try to disguise. But since the day she arrived, he had never once mentioned sharing a bedroom, let alone marriage. She understood that he was enticing her, using every one of his persuasive skills to enchant her, but she couldn't bring herself to care because this was the Alessandro she knew from Nice, the man who had charmed her with no end goal. Before he abruptly ended all contact, she reminded herself. She couldn't forget that piece.

She was going along with this for the baby, she told herself. All of this pleasure, and all these leisurely, drawn-out evenings lingering by the table must be doing something to lower her high blood pressure. And then she would return to Stockholm. But the idea of looking out her apartment window into the gray autumn skies as the daylight grew shorter felt so far away, and Alessandro's teasing voice, his soft, sensual caresses, his laughter—it was all so very present. So she tried not to think too hard about the fact that the end was coming closer.

One evening, as the sunset turned the sky bright oranges and reds and made the leaves on row after row of grapevines shimmer, Alessandro pulled the lounge chairs to the edge of the terrace to watch Mother Nature's evening show.

"Tell me about the kind of life you would like when the baby comes," he said softly, seriously.

This life. She almost spoke the thought aloud. But the life she imagined here was with Alessandro, and she was almost sure this life had limits they would run into at any time. So instead, she imagined herself back in Stockholm. "I have paid maternity leave for over a year, so I imagine there will be plenty of diapers and feeding and walks in the park."

Over the last seven months, she had passed countless

mothers with prams in Vasaparken, and yet she still couldn't picture herself doing the same. It felt so unreal.

"Is that what you want?" His voice was soft, and there was something guarded in his expression.

She swallowed. "Honestly, I don't think parenting a newborn has much to do with what I want."

The corners of his full mouth quirked up at the wryness in her voice.

"Point taken," he said. Then his smile faded. "I still think you should ask yourself this question."

She tried to ask it that night as she lay in bed, with the sweet caresses of Alessandro's lips still lingering. But after years of separating want from need, it felt wrong. As if just thinking about her wants was asking too much.

After a week, she and Alessandro stood in a spacious examination room in a doctor's office, taking in their surroundings. Alessandro had tempted her into walking to the appointment with a promise of a stop at a café in the main palazzo for her new favorite midmorning snack, a decaffeinated cappuccino and a fresh pastry from the bakery. The doctor's office was just off the palazzo in a majestic stone building with tall windows and stone gargoyles guarding from the top floor. As they had wandered in, she had expected to find the same sort of evidence of times past that she had seen in all of the town's shops, as if the building was etched with a history of the comings and goings of the little town's residents.

But the inside of the doctor's office was nothing like anything she had seen in town. It looked newly renovated and startlingly well-equipped for a village practice in the rural countryside. When she glanced at Alessandro, he was studying her as if trying to read her.

"The doctor will come to the villa at any time, of course, but she suggested a visit at the office, where she had the ultrasound machine and any other equipment she might need at hand," he said.

Her surprise turned to amusement. "I have been to countless doctor's appointments during my pregnancy, and not once have I considered the possibility of a doctor coming to me. I'm perfectly fine with an office visit." Her gaze drifted to the computers and machines that filled the place. "I just can't believe that a small town would have the same services that were in the hospital in the center of Stockholm. This place seems prepared for anything."

Alessandro gave a little nod. "When Massimo and I were young, my grandmother made a long-term commitment to significantly boost the finances of this place. The equipment, building upkeep, bonuses for the staff, whatever they needed."

She blinked. "That was quite generous of her."

"In a way." His expression turned darker. "My grandmother took over some of my father's business roles so he could focus more on his family. When she understood that Massimo and I would be here without the attention of our parents, she switched tactics and built up the community around us to help."

She looked around her at the fully equipped office. "But this is for everyone. She could have just hired a doctor."

"I think she understood that we were a handful, and the task she needed required more than money. Quite frankly, I think she wanted the town to have an incentive to take care of us."

She tilted her head to the side a little. "Maybe that qualifies as self-interested, but this whole town has a state-of-the-art practice. Good has come from it."

He flashed her a wry smile. "I guess all this money does have its uses."

A knock on the door saved her from coming up with a good response to that. A woman with long, graying hair walked in.

"Dr. Cantabella," said Alessandro, and their embrace was warm and familiar.

The doctor shook Ann-Sophie's hand. "I received your medical charts from Stockholm, and I noted the high-blood-pressure readings. Your doctor reported no other complications."

Out of the corner of her eye, Alessandro seemed to stiffen at the mention of her high blood pressure.

"That's correct," said Ann-Sophie, "if you don't count the problem getting in and out of chairs."

Dr. Cantabella smiled.

"I'm hoping a few weeks in Italy have helped to bring my blood pressure down," she added.

"Let's check." Ann-Sophie could feel herself tense the way she always did these days when thinking about her blood pressure…likely triggering higher blood pressure. The doctor seemed to recognize this problem. "Try closing your eyes and imagining yourself somewhere else, a favorite place."

She loved to travel so her favorite place changed all the time, but right now, the place that came to her was her favorite alcove in the library with two velvet seats. She pictured it in detail, the light filtering through the stained glass, the scents of thousands of books, all waiting to be explored. But she wasn't alone. In this vision, Alessandro was there, so close, leaning over her to kiss her and then…

"Your blood pressure looks good," said the doctor with a note of surprise in her voice. "I'm not sure what you imagined but your heartbeat went up at the end of the reading."

Ann-Sophie flushed, but the doctor smiled at her. "Whatever you're doing, it's working."

She let out an audible sigh. She glanced over Alessandro and saw glimpses of relief and happiness.

"Let's check on the little one," said Dr. Cantabella, then rolled the ultrasound machine from the corner.

Ann-Sophie exposed her growing belly, and she could see the way Alessandro's eyes were drawn to it. His expression stayed neutral, but she could've sworn that she saw a flash of desire in his eyes before it shifted into something more appropriate.

As the doctor moved the wand over her stomach, images took shape on the monitor. A nose. Lips. A foot with tiny toes. Their baby. It was there, moving, its tiny body curled, protected inside her. A burst of joy took over, and she turned to meet Alessandro's gaze, to share this moment with him, but all the lightness of the past few moments had disappeared.

His expression was stark, and the haunted look in his

eyes cut a hole in her own happiness. The bubbling joy that had run through her just moments ago was leaking out of her so fast she didn't know what to do with it.

"The baby looks wonderful," gushed Dr. Cantabella, startling Ann-Sophie out of her thoughts. She tried to focus on the monitor, but the feeling this visit had just taken a very bad turn stayed with her. The doctor seemed oblivious. "Please continue with your blood-pressure monitoring and come back in a week, but don't hesitate to call or come in before that with any questions."

Never once had a doctor or midwife been this solicitous, and yet Ann-Sophie barely heard these generous offers. All she could think about was the haunted look in Alessandro's eyes.

They exited the modern insides of the doctor's office and started down the steps to the cobblestone street. As they walked across the palazzo, he asked, "Would you like to walk home, or should I call for a car?"

"Walk," she said. A ride involved a driver, and right now, she wanted to be alone with him.

As they started up the hilly streets, he slipped his hand in hers, but there was no connection. It was as if he had simply turned it off.

Finally, she pulled her hand from his and came to a stop. "What happened in the doctor's office?"

Alessandro was wearing sunglasses, but she was almost sure he wasn't looking at her. "I don't know what you're talking about."

She was sure he did. "When you saw the baby, something happened."

He shook his head and began to walk again. As they continued along the street, Ann-Sophie could feel her frustration growing. They were on the edge of town with a few scattered buildings, and the gate into the villa wasn't far ahead. She stopped again. He looked up at the gate, then back at her.

"Let's continue." His voice was now filled with warning.

"No." The word came out stronger than she had expected. "Something happened and it was about the baby."

He grimaced, as if she had slapped him.

"You need to think about your blood pressure," he said. She could see the way his jaw clenched as he spoke these words in a low voice.

She threw up her hands. "Is this a version of telling me to 'calm down'? Because that doesn't work. You need to think about the child."

The words slipped out of her mouth before she thought about how harsh they sounded. She closed her eyes. *Deep, calming breaths.* When she opened them, Alessandro had removed his sunglasses, and his expression was stark. In his eyes she saw fury and pain. "I'm *always* thinking about the child. I can promise you that."

Her breath caught at the graveness in his voice. It rattled through her, the rebuke a slash inside. She swallowed. "I'm sorry. That came out wrong. I didn't mean it that way."

A little of the hardness in his eyes softened. She searched for more words, but nothing seemed right.

"Explain this to me," she finally whispered. "*Please.*"

With the word *please*, his eyes softened a little more. He didn't speak. He looked out in the countryside and she wondered what he was thinking about right now, what he saw in this place and what he saw in her. The distance between them had suddenly widened, and it felt like she would never understand him. The thought weighed heavily inside her.

When he looked at her again, something had shifted. In his eyes, she found familiar spark of heat, and it sent a distracting jolt of awareness through her. "We'll talk back at the villa."

Something had loosened inside of Alessandro in the doctor's office, and it was not settling back the way it should have. The way he needed it to. Instead, he felt the ominous echoes of his younger years, when everything around him seem to trigger a live wire inside him, jolting him with feelings he couldn't process. He had deadened that live wire long ago, or at least he thought he had, but staring at the image of the baby... The bones of his long-buried emotions had rattled to life again, and they threatened everything that he had spent his adult life building.

But Alessandro knew how to fix this. He knew exactly what would channel all these emotions into something that brought temporary relief and not destruction. He had resisted this path for over a week, focusing on the most strategic way forward to marriage, but ignoring his own needs was clearly taking its toll. Because he was not a man who was accustomed to depriving himself, not in this way. He thrived on sensual indulgence, and the woman in front of him was indulgence incarnate. If this situation was going to demand a pound of flesh from him, he would take from it the pleasures of flesh in return.

Alessandro led Ann-Sophie up the path to the villa and through the silent halls of his childhood, past doors he used to peek through, looking for his absent parents, long before he understood that they were not hiding in one of the countless rooms of this villa, but had fled to someplace or another with half-formed excuses. Over the years, they dropped the pretense of reasons for their disappearances, leaving it to Olivia to deliver the news. *The way you did to Ann-Sophie.* The thought rattled inside him, and he shoved it away.

As they continued past the hall to what had been his childhood room, he felt the urge to pause. It was strange. He had not dwelled on this part of his life since Ann-Sophie had arrived. But she seemed to infuse unexpected joy into the place where shadows always lurked. Now, all these memories were crashing down on him. He needed to staunch his wounds before they bled him dry. But first, he would give her what she wanted, a glimpse into the past that had formed him. And then he would ask for what he wanted in return.

Alessandro led them through the halls and came to a stop in front of the door next to her room.

"You really have been sleeping on the other side of the wall from me this whole time?" she asked.

He tucked a strand of silky hair behind her ear, then

whispered, "Every night, I imagined what we would do if you came to find me."

Her cheeks flushed a satisfying pink. The lavender scent of her hair was everywhere, and her plump lips were parted and so temptingly close. Just a little more patience, he told himself. When he opened the door, she looked up at him, then entered.

The room was decorated with rich tapestries and hand-carved furniture, and Alessandro appreciated these more impersonal qualities. It lacked the specific associations that his childhood room had.

She stood before a painting of a bacchanalian scene. "Whose room was this? It couldn't have been yours as a boy."

"It was intended for guests, though it hasn't seen any in quite a few years."

She wandered around the room, and he followed her, like an animal closing in on his prey, his eyes drawn to the curves of her full breasts spilling over the bodice of her sundress. When she had finished peering in the closets and pausing at the bookshelves, he gestured to the baroque love seat.

"Please, sit."

Ann-Sophie settled into the little sofa, and Alessandro found a footrest for her to prop up her feet, then sat next to her. He stared at the spray of freckles that had darkened across her nose over the last week in the sun. This life here in his villa suited her, he thought, clinging to the satisfaction the thought gave him.

But before he could let the heat of their closeness distract him, he would give her what she asked for.

Honesty. It was an exchange, one he had to make for the outcome he needed, he reminded himself. Soon, this would all be over.

Her eyes lost a little of their hazy focus. "What happened in the doctor's office? I don't know how to describe it. You looked almost…" Her lips curved down into a frown. "You looked haunted when you saw our child. Whatever this is, we need to discuss it before the baby is born."

The words sent tremors through the control he had clawed back, but he gave her a tight smile. "I have my questions about being the father that I want to be, and seeing the baby reminded me of them."

This was all true. Or at least the most palatable version of the truth.

Her frown deepened. "Is this related to what you said about your parents?"

He knew this wasn't an intentional jab, and yet he felt barbs dig into him. "Are you feeling sorry for this poor little rich boy?"

His voice was smooth and cutting, laced with mockery. It happened so quickly, a reflex that he regretted. He wanted to take this woman to bed and marry her, and yet he found himself snapping at her. And they hadn't even begun to get into the details. It made no sense, but this was the problem, wasn't it? This was why he had built up his walls.

Her eyes widened, but to her credit, she didn't shrink away.

"Don't do that," she said with a steadiness he hadn't expected.

Alessandro gritted his teeth and reined in that out-of-control feeling inside him. He *would not* lash out again. Cruelty was straight out of his mother's playbook, and he would not be like his mother. Not at any price.

"I'm sorry," he said quietly, then forced himself to go on. "When Massimo and I were in our teens, we didn't last long at any of our boarding schools. Our records say we both got kicked out for fighting, but that is not quite the truth. I got into fights, and Massimo backed me up.

"Something small would trigger me, my anger was suddenly overwhelming. I would let it out, and, of course, people would come back at me. Massimo and I had always been athletic, and we were raised feral in a way that our upper-class classmates weren't used to, so taking on a couple of them wasn't a problem. But pride is a powerful motivator at these places, so inevitably there was retaliation, and Massimo took my side. Even my grandparents' money and prestige weren't enough to keep us there."

That part was easier to talk about because everyone he went to school with knew it. The next part was harder.

"When we got kicked out the first time, I expected my parents to pick us up and berate us. As it turned out, they couldn't be bothered. We simply got shipped directly to a new school. But after the third expulsion, we were finally delivered somewhere else—our grandparents' estate.

"That alone should have been enough to change my

course, but I was a handful, wild, getting into all sorts of trouble with anyone I could find. Usually, my grandmother's lectures were given at the table, so I was surprised one day when I found my grandmother waiting for me one last night as I sulked in the door. She looked at me and said, 'Your parents are not going to come no matter how much trouble you cause or don't cause. You cannot let this anger control you. You must control it or neither you nor your brother will have a future.'"

The fear those words had triggered still sent a chill through him today, but he was too far into this story to stop here.

"I think she knew if she had told me my own future was doomed, I wouldn't have listened. But my brother, the better twin, a smart, ambitious one—that I could and would destroy him? The idea filled me with a kind of fear I had never experienced before."

Ann-Sophie frowned at him, as if she was missing something. "What do you mean by the better twin?"

"When I was younger, my parents told me this in countless ways. I was too loud, my tantrums were driving them crazy and dyslexia was just a badge of incompetence to them. I was a disappointment and made things hard for them. And if my memory serves correctly, there was some truth to that."

He felt numb as he said these words, but when he caught a glimpse of the devastation in her expression, something twisted inside.

Her brow furrowed. "But most eight-year-olds cause their parents grief. I caused my mother plenty of heartache."

Something flickered in her gaze and he was drawn back to her story.

"But wanting to know about one's father is a natural thing," he protested. "That's not the same."

She tilted her head to the side a little. "Isn't wanting your parents' attention natural, too?"

"Not in the way that I did it. Massimo, for example, managed to get through this without, for example, throwing a piece of priceless art at the wall, chosen specifically because my mother had just bought it."

Ann-Sophie looked at him as if she wanted to disagree but held herself back. "So you went to your grandparents and had a good conversation and that fixed it?"

He wanted to tell her yes, but she had that skeptical look on her face, and he wanted to get through the conversation as quickly as he could. He wanted this to be finished.

"I found a more acceptable outlet for my emotions," he said evenly.

She raised her eyebrows. "I'm curious to hear a teenage boy's boundaries of acceptable."

He laughed, despite all the heaviness he felt. "Teenage boys are not particularly known for acceptable boundaries, nor for their emotional awareness."

The corners of her mouth lifted.

"It's tempting to make something up just to shock you," he said. "But you will probably be able to guess where I found my solution, considering that it is at the heart of my well-earned reputation."

Her brow furrowed again for a moment, but then understanding seem to hit her. “Sex.”

He nodded, and she was quiet, as if this idea was sinking in. He let her put together these pieces of him. Part of him regretted telling her this, as she would likely soon understand her own unwitting role in this portrait. But showing her these parts of himself was part of larger negotiations, he reminded himself. Even if this conversation felt like something completely different.

Finally, she gave him a look that bordered on amusement. “So basically, in Nice I was part of a long-term self-styled therapy project to keep your emotions under control?”

He could smooth over the hint of bleakness in her voice and get her to laugh, and this could lead them to what his body was craving. He could have brushed it off, telling himself he had imagined it, but something wouldn’t let him do it. He told himself to follow his business instincts, that he was so close to getting what he wanted, but…

It would hurt her. And he couldn’t make himself do that.

So instead, he gave her a self-mocking smile. “It was supposed to be like an alternative to therapy. But it isn’t supposed to affect others, and with my well-earned reputation usually comes an understanding that there are limits to a fling with me.”

“I’m afraid I didn’t follow your exploits closely enough to get that message,” she said, the sharpness returning to her voice.

He shook his head impatiently. "That wasn't the problem. Others have asked for more, and I have gently, smoothly, led them back to an appropriate understanding. But with you, I didn't. I *couldn't*. I had a reaction and I have spent the last seven months trying to figure out why."

Ann-Sophie blinked, as if this was the last thing she had expected him to say. Then her eyes narrowed, as if she didn't believe him.

"It was why I blocked your number," he added, his voice rising. "It was why I never answered your message. It would have been so easy to slowly let you down the way I, frankly, have done to other women. But even on that last night, I knew if we had any further contact, it would make giving you up harder. So… I took precautions."

"Because we never had a chance? You never imagined anything more with me?"

He knew the answer she wanted, but he couldn't make himself give it to her. It would be a lie. "I have made sure never to imagine anything more with anyone."

"I see." Her voice was a whisper.

"Until now."

The silence that hung between them felt uneasy, precarious. He had just tipped his hand instead of playing his best card, and she could decide what to do with it. And still, *still*, he felt the pull of her body, the longing that had been building since the moment he had seen her in front of her apartment building. And he wanted her like nothing he had ever wanted in his life. He wanted to soothe the riot of feelings that were threatening to take over, but he held himself still, his fingers tense with the effort of not pressing his lips to hers, losing himself in her, and letting all other thoughts disappear.

She lifted her hand and ran it over his cheek, and when he met her gaze, he could see the understanding was mixed with determination. Did she think she could save him? Change him? Did she think this scenario had a happy ending, where he would get over his past and they would live happily ever after? If so, she was not the first to make the mistake. It had happened enough times that he understood this as a warning sign.

He should back away, but at his core he was a deeply selfish man, and some things just would never change. He knew this would create problems further down the road, but he reminded himself he had tried to do the right thing and it still had led him here. So he gave in. He leaned into the lush temptation of her lips and kissed her.

CHAPTER SEVEN

I HAVE MADE sure never to imagine anything more with anyone. Until now.

Alessandro's words looped through Ann-Sophie's brain as his mouth pressed against her for an achingly slow kiss. Her heart pounded in her chest, and it felt as if her body was floating. His kisses were both too much and somehow not enough, and desperation tinged her hunger for him.

I could spend forever right here, in this moment. The thought was startling, overwhelming, but before she could process it, she was suddenly in his arms and he was lifting her, belly and all.

"Where are you taking me?"

The intensity of his gaze was dizzying. "The place I've wanted you since the day I brought you here."

He set her down in the middle of an imposing bed of thick dark wood, but instead of following, he got on his knees in front of her. Alessandro was *kneeling* before her. Slowly, he removed one shoe, then another.

"Thanks. My shoes are hard to reach these days," she said, trying to lighten the mood and this feeling of enormity of the moment.

Alessandro smiled a little. "I am so happy to be of service, as always."

This was the man who had seduced her in Nice, and she felt a sudden twist of disappointment as their conversation from just moments ago came together with this moment. For him this was a road to forgetting, not connecting. How did that fit with imagining something more?

She told herself it didn't have to all make sense right now, not when she wanted him like this. She had wanted him so many times this week but was afraid of what would happen if she gave in, but now, she had decided to put her fears aside and have him. That thought disappeared when he began to lift her dress, revealing her body. Fear broke through the haze of desire. He hadn't reacted well to the ultrasound of the baby. What would he do when he saw the full extent of her bare belly? It wasn't easily overlooked.

"Are you sure you want to see…all of me?"

His dark eyes glittered. "Very sure."

Then she remembered the way he had looked at her in the pool, with a kind of hunger that suggested that he desired her as she was, right now. But the fear that he would suddenly turn on her, reject her, abandon her—it still lingered, and she didn't know how to make it go away.

He lifted her sundress again, this time exposing the roundness of her belly, and she stilled as he settled his hands on it. The baby moved, and she saw him flinch, but he didn't pull away. Maybe this was what he needed, she told herself, just a period of getting used to the idea of having a child. After all, she had had seven months to get used to it, and Alessandro had had little over a week. She couldn't expect him to seamlessly blend the idea of a baby into his life so quickly, could she? Of course, there would be these little bumps in the road.

They could move forward. She wanted to move forward when being with him felt this good. Maybe if she gave all of this a real chance, their little family could be everything she wanted it to be. Right now, everything was possible.

The tight coil of desire was building inside her, spreading languid heat through her limbs. Alessandro unfastened the top button of his crisp, white shirt, revealing bronze skin and a hint of dark hair. He unbuttoned another and another, each button revealing more of the flat planes of his chest, then his muscular abs, as Ann-Sophie stood, mesmerized. He shrugged off his shirt, his biceps flexing, a reminder of the power and strength her body remembered. He unbuttoned his pants, and her heart thudded relentlessly in her chest as the last of his clothes slid down his body. Alessandro stood in front of her very naked and very aroused. This man was a god, with burnished muscles and the infinite complexities of light and darkness. *And he could be hers forever.*

"I asked the doctor if this was safe when I made the appointment, and she said as long as you are comfortable, we are free to do what we like." He flashed her a smile. "I intend to aim a bit higher than comfortable."

He propped pillows on the top of his bed, then gestured for her to lie back on them. The mattress dipped as he climbed between her legs.

"You have no idea how sexy I find you," he said, his voice a low groan.

She lifted one eyebrow and gestured to her round belly. "Even like this?"

"Especially like this," he said, and the low rumble of his voice left no doubt in her mind that he was telling the truth. But attraction had always been their connection, not an obstacle that spread the distance between them.

Suddenly, she wanted him with a desperation that took her breath away. Memories of Nice were a montage of sex and laughter and insatiable want, and they flooded through her mind, finally free.

She propped herself up on her elbows and bit her lip.

"How do we do this now?" she said, gesturing again to her belly.

Alessandro crawled up her body, his torso skimming her belly as he moved, and smug satisfaction was written across his face. "We'll figure it out."

Then he brought his mouth to one breast, and all rational thought left her. Her nipples had become more sensitive as the baby had grown, and the moment he put his mouth on her, she felt a jolt of overwhelming pleasure that was somehow connected to that place between her legs. She cried out and he pulled back.

"Does that not feel good?" he asked, frowning, his gaze focused.

"It does. It's just…a lot." She swallowed, then smiled. "I haven't done this in seven months."

Some of the humor left his face as he looked at her. “Neither have I.”

Ann-Sophie blinked, registering words that rattled through her. They were chased with another burst of hope, this one stronger than the last. *Everything was possible.* But then his mouth was on her other breast, this time a slow tease, and she was lost in that delicious building pleasure. She let out a soft gasp, and he moved lower, kissing a trail down her stomach.

He slid off her panties and urged her legs open, and then he kissed a line up one of her legs. Her breath caught in her throat. Alessandro was kissing her inside her knee, up her thigh, on her stomach, and then finally, finally between her legs. The sensation exploded through her. It had been so very long, and she trembled under the slow caresses of his mouth. Her legs fell open, and she whimpered in pleasure, both familiar and new. Alessandro let out a low groan, then continued his slow, exacting assault on her senses. She was gasping for air, crying out at the pleasure until ecstasy exploded inside her, too much to hold back. He caressed her slowly, drawing out her pleasure, as her body sank into bliss.

“I’m so sensitive now,” she whispered with a husky laugh.

She opened her eyes and found Alessandro watching her with what looked like primal satisfaction. “I noticed. I knew I would enjoy these changes to your body.”

He crawled next to her on the bed and lay down behind her, stroking her arms, her waist. He kissed her neck with a tenderness that made her ache inside. And when he pressed his hips against her, she welcomed his hard, insistent length. Desire surged inside her again, and in that moment, she wondered if she would ever stop wanting this man. But then he slid his long, thick length inside her, and she was lost again.

He let out a long, low groan, and she had the urge to turn around, to see the pleasure on his face, to feel the connection, the intimacy that she hadn't let herself think about. Because she remembered the way it had felt to look into his eyes when he was inside her. Every barrier between them had slipped away. She hadn't let herself think about this in seven months and yet now, she wanted it desperately. But he was behind her, and when she turned a little, he gently pressed his hand on her cheek and kissed her neck again. Maybe it meant nothing, but she couldn't help but wonder if he was turning her away from him.

But even this thought disappeared when he began to move, his long length stroking the most sensitive parts inside her, and she gasped and cried as he taunted her with pleasure and teased her until she was there at the precipice again. As he pushed her over, she heard herself cry out his name. Then with a long, low grown, he came inside of her. The room was filled with the sound of their breaths as they lay there, connected. He kept his arm around her, his chest warm and solid against her back, and in that moment, she was happy. This life Alessandro was showing her was more than most people could ever hope for. It was pleasure and security for the baby. It would mean both parents would be a part of the child's life.

And in exchange, Alessandro wanted marriage.

It was not the marriage she had foreseen for herself. But maybe she should try for the baby.

She shifted, turning on the bed until she was facing him. Alessandro looked lost in less upbeat thoughts, but when she met his gaze, some of the heaviness faded. She leaned forward to kiss him.

"What would it look like if we married?" she asked quietly.

He blinked, as if the question caught him off guard. "What do you want it to look like?"

"I want to raise the child in Stockholm, at least some of the time."

"You're not enjoying the luxuries of this life?" He traced the curve of his arm with his fingers.

"I want us to have a more…typical life."

"The baby is not typical. Nothing about being a Carandini is typical."

She smiled a little. "I've noticed."

"This is a lovely place to raise a child, part-time. The child will have you and Olivia…"

"And you?"

"When I can get away."

"I see."

He was quiet for a moment. "You will have my resources at your disposal, and we will have a life together. I can give you pleasure and company, but I cannot give you love."

Ann-Sophie ignored the sting of this comment. “Of course.”

“You’re not asking for love?”

She hesitated. Neither of them knew what the future held. A week ago, she hadn’t expected this moment. But right now. *Everything was possible.*

“I don’t expect love,” she said carefully.

He met her gaze again, studying her, and for a moment it felt as if the wall between them fell away. He found her hand and laced his fingers with hers. “Ann-Sophie, will you marry me?”

For once in her life, she allowed herself to *want*.

“Yes,” she whispered. “I will marry you.”

The next week flew by in a flurry of plans and paperwork. The wedding would take place in two weeks, a little after the baby hit the eight-month mark, giving them a little space before the delivery date. It would be a small affair in the village church, and the only invitees would be Massimo and Catarina, who had insisted on coming, and Ann-Sophie’s mother, if she could make it.

Ann-Sophie looked thoughtful when he suggested it. “But I think she’s away on assignment.”

“I’m sure she’ll come back for your wedding.”

“But it’s such a small thing and the baby is almost here. Maybe I should ask her to come for the birth instead.”

Alessandro found that he didn’t like the way that she so readily made excuses for why her mother didn’t need to be there, but he said nothing.

"If I'm telling my mother, then you should let your parents know, too." She lifted an eyebrow. "Or maybe you don't want to invite your parents?"

"It doesn't matter either way," he said darkly. "They won't come. But I'll have Massimo pass on the message."

There were documents to prepare and a prenup to sign, one that specified dual residences in Stockholm and Italy. It made generous provisions for her and the baby under a single condition.

"'As long as the baby is biologically yours?'" she said, reading aloud. Then she looked up at him with narrowed eyes. "I don't even know where to begin with this line."

This topic was infinitely frustrating, and Alessandro felt the control inside him start to crack. "You would not perform a DNA test. You're leaving me with no choice."

"Interesting definition of 'no choice,'" she said, rolling her eyes.

The fissure lines inside him spread ominously.

"Why are you choosing to dig in your heels about this issue?" he demanded.

Ann-Sophie glanced at the lawyer, standing at the edge of the desk and pretending not to listen, like he was paid to do.

"Because it means you still don't trust me," she said softly.

Alessandro swiped a hand over his face, exasperated. "You're making this more complicated than it has to be. If the baby is mine, then we have no problem."

"I don't think this is complicated at all. Either you trust the woman that you are about to marry or you do not."

The fissure lines inside threatened to break. He had kept his emotions perfectly under control over the last week. She had moved into his bedroom, and they spent their days together, making love at all hours. Everything about this was exactly as it should be. But she wanted more.

"Trust is not easy for me, even under less pressing circumstances," he said, his jaw tight. "I need this from you."

"Fine," she said, turning away, and her voice was cold and distant. "I'll sign it."

He stared at her, waiting for the familiar satisfaction in this win. He had softened Ann-Sophie by giving her pleasure and the emotional vulnerability that was driving him to the brink of his sanity, and he was now reaping the rewards. His plan was an irrefutable success, and he searched for the familiar rush that success always brought. It didn't come.

All he could think about was the way she wouldn't look at him right now. And the chill of her voice, as if he'd ruined everything. As if he was now the bully that he had never wanted to be.

That evening, she was quiet. The moon cast its watchful eye on them, reflecting off the ripples of the pool, as if to reflect every moment of the strain the afternoon had put on them. As they sipped the last of their evening coffee and ate the last bites of almond cake that Olivia had baked, Ann-Sophie turned to him.

"I realize I gave you a reason not to trust me. It was wrong of me not to tell you for seven months about the pregnancy. But do you really think I would lie about the baby's paternity?"

He closed his eyes. "I don't. But a baby does not change me as a person. It does not take away thirty-one years of carefully guarding whom I trust." *This is who I am.* It was meant as a warning.

And yet she didn't take it as one because she smiled, so beautifully and inexplicably. "Alessandro Carandini… changing? Impossible."

It was the first time she had smiled at him since the papers were signed, and he found himself reveling in it.

"It does sound quite improbable, doesn't it?" he mused.

She shook her head slowly, but her smile grew, and suddenly everything felt lighter. Alessandro tipped his head back and looked at the stars that glowed in the night sky. What would it be like to hold on to this lightness, to share it with Ann-Sophie? And though he knew he was entering dangerous territory, right now, he wanted for this to be possible. Real.

That was the stuff of dreams. But the two of them were inextricably tied to reality, which he had to focus on.

So he turned to her and gave her his most charming smile. "I would like us to attend an event in a few days in Rome. It will be the official introduction of you as my wife."

She blinked, as if she hadn't considered this angle of being the husband of Alessandro Carandini and the mother of a Carandini heir. "What do I have to do?"

"Just be yourself."

Ann-Sophie gave a charming little snort of laughter. "Why am I getting the feeling it won't be that simple?"

CHAPTER EIGHT

"I'M GETTING MARRIED."

"Married?" Ann-Sophie's mother's voice flickered in and out on the other end of the line. Margarita Svensson was in Ethiopia, reporting on coffee beans that still grew wild in the mountain jungle and the farmers that harvested them. Gorgeous location, thought-provoking discussions, but tenuous mobile service at best.

"Yes. *Married*." Ann-Sophie emphasized the word.

"To whom?"

"The father of the baby." It was a testament to her state of mind for the first seven months of this pregnancy that her mother needed to ask.

"I thought you hadn't spoken with him because he was an—" The connection broke off, but her mother's message was not lost.

"He was. But things feel different now." This reasoning sounded weaker when she spoke it aloud, but it *did* feel different.

"Are you sure that you want to marry him?"

She stared down at the enormous diamond ring he'd slipped on her finger with a seriousness that she hadn't expected. *From my grandmother*, he had said, his eyes guarded.

This was not a marriage built on love, she had reminded herself.

But still, the answer rang inside of her: She wanted to marry Alessandro. She didn't need it, but she wanted it. The problem was that she couldn't stop hoping the marriage would be anchored in something more, no matter how many times Alessandro implied it would be about creating a family. And having a lot of sex, if the past few days were any indication. She was definitely not going to get into this with her mother, so instead she said, "I think this is the best choice for the baby. I want the baby to grow up around both of us."

"You didn't answer my question." But then her mother gave a laugh. "You've always been such an independent child. Who am I to tell you how to live your life?"

The words warmed her. The last thing Ann-Sophie wanted was for her mother to feel like she had been a burden. When her mother had taught her to differentiate between want and need, it had allowed Ann-Sophie to be the kind of child that left her mother free to have some of the kind of life she had before Ann-Sophie came along. It was the least she could do for her mother.

"When is the wedding?"

"In a week," she said. Then, in the silence, she quickly added, "It will just be a short ceremony. No party. Really, a small thing. You don't need to come."

There was another pause on the line, and then her mother said, "Okay. Well, please send me pictures."

"I will," she said. "I love you."

"I love you more than you can imagine." The words came through like patchwork, and Ann-Sophie clung to them after the line died. She lay back on the bed she now shared with Alessandro, telling herself that her mother shouldn't come all the way from Ethiopia just for a wedding that was for the baby, not a fairy tale about love. Even if Alessandro did resemble a fairy-tale prince with an *actual castle*.

The next morning, they left for Rome.

As they drove to the airport, where Alessandro's jet waited, Ann-Sophie thought about how much had changed since they had driven on this road for the first time weeks ago. She was marrying this sexy, enigmatic man next to her, and they were going to an event of the kind she had only attended for work. This time, she was a guest. Alessandro Carandini's fiancée. She would leave the other attendees with no doubt as to the reasons behind this surprise engagement, she thought wryly as she caressed her stomach. *It's all for you*, she whispered to her baby.

"Is your mother coming to the wedding?" asked Alessandro, as the family's jet skirted the coast of Italy, the jagged shoreline on one side, the glittering sea on the other.

Ann-Sophie shook her head. "She has so much going on."

Alessandro frowned but said nothing.

She raised an eyebrow. "Why? Are your parents coming?"

He gave a humorless laugh. "My mother is cruel,

and my father's image is more important than anything else. They are the last people we want at our wedding."

"I see," she said, though she wasn't sure she did.

The flight to Rome was short, and when they landed, they were whisked away in a black limousine and delivered to the Hotel de la Ville in the center of town. The lobby was a cool relief from the hot Roman sun, and its black-and-white marble floors shone in the light of the chandeliers.

"It's wonderful to see you again, Signore Carandini," said the woman checking them in, then she glanced at Ann-Sophie. "I have you in the Roma suite, as usual."

As usual. Ann-Sophie tried not to think about the other guests that had visited him in this suite over the years. Alessandro had talked about his past with women in such an impersonal way that she hadn't thought much of it. At the villa, they had their own world, the one they could make their own. But they were far from the secluded life of the villa. Here, Alessandro had a name for himself, a tabloid reputation that she was stepping into. She wasn't sure how she was going to deal with that.

They rode the elevator to the top floor, and an intricately carved red door waited for them at the end of the hallway. They entered into a living room with sofas, a writing desk and abstract art in muted colors. French doors led out to a balcony that overlooked the tall, elegant city buildings, partly obscured by cypress trees. On the coffee table was a tray of drink options and another filled with meats, cheeses, olives, apricots and different spreads for the small loaf of bread.

"I called ahead to make sure you and the baby don't go hungry, as supper will be served late at this event."

She grabbed a handful of spiced almonds. "First, I need to find a dress."

She had tried on her only maternity dress that came close to being suitable and found that she had already outgrown it. In the last three weeks.

"I took the liberty of ordering a selection of dresses, shoes and intimate wear." His eyes flared with desire at these last words, and he gestured to the doorway into the bedroom. "If you don't find anything you like, we can send out for a new selection."

Ann-Sophie blinked in surprise. She knew personal shopping services existed, and that people like Alessandro lived the kind of life where things were delivered at their convenience, but she still couldn't quite get used to the fact that *she* was living that life. A life where questions of need versus want were irrelevant because she could have both. Alessandro would give her whatever she wanted. *Except the thing you want the most from him*, said a voice deep inside her.

"Thank you," she said and entered the bedroom. The suite was located on the corner of the building, and light poured into the long tall windows that looked out at the ancient buildings that surrounded them. The shadows of leaves filtered the light in ripples across the white bedspread.

Ann-Sophie crossed the elegant room and opened up the armoire. Inside, it was filled with silky dresses, all floor-length but in different colors with different necklines, and at the bottom were stacks of shoeboxes.

She ran her fingers over the selection, touching the soft materials. Of course, nothing so gauche as a price tag was in sight. It was all so unreal. She stared at the rainbow of colors and finally picked a light blue dress made of soft silk, the color of her eyes. She slipped off her cotton sundress, one that had miraculously turned up in her wardrobe shortly after arrival, and let the soft silk slip over her body. It fit perfectly. The low *V* emphasized the extra fullness in her breasts, and the gathered material spilled over her baby bump and hung in shimmering waves. She turned to search for a mirror and found Alessandro standing in the doorway. He was leaning in the threshold, his crisp white shirt rolled at the sleeves and his hands in his pockets. His eyes were heavy with desire. She flushed with awareness as a slow smile curved on his lips.

"That one. Definitely."

She walked into the large bathroom suite and stood in front of the full-length mirror. It was so flashy and it definitely highlighted her belly. For the first time since her body had started its accelerated expansion, she felt…beautiful.

"I love it," she said.

Alessandro came up behind her, and his hands skimmed over her arms as he stared at her image in the mirror.

"We'll need to find more places to wear this, *cara*," he said and brushed a kiss on her neck.

She laughed. "Let's see how this evening goes before we make plans for future appearances."

He met her gaze in the mirror, and his smile turned

darker. "You will be by my side in this gown. There's nothing else that I want out of this evening."

The words sent a rush of that dangerous, giddy hope she had felt too often this week. When he said things like this, she couldn't stop herself from hoping this could be about more than just the baby and physical attraction. Maybe they could find their way to the kind of *more* she shouldn't think about. Because the real version of fairy tales with castles and princes didn't have happy endings, she reminded herself. They were much more complicated.

The afternoon was a flurry of hairstylists and makeup artists and lounging on the long, surprisingly comfortable sofa, as Alessandro answered calls and plied her with food from the generous trays. And by the time they sat in the limo on their way to the gala, Ann-Sophie was starting to think maybe she could get used to this life. Even if it did not seem attached to any sort of reality she had known.

When they pulled up to the Borghese Gallery, her breath caught in her throat at the spectacular display in front of them. A long red carpet made a trail down the center of the walkway to the entrance, and it was lit by tall votive candles on both sides. In front of them, stately pillars glittered with lights in the dusky sunset.

And then there was the paparazzi. She had attended events at locations like this, but she and her fellow interpreters were treated like extras in a movie, the backdrop for those who mattered. This time, she would be noticed. Photographed and assessed.

Alessandro helped her out of the limousine and

laced his large, warm hand with hers as they started along the red carpet. His bespoke tuxedo emphasized his broad shoulders and solid strength, but the unruly curl of his hair was a reminder of the humor that set him apart from his twin brother. Her heart pounded as she glanced up at this breathtaking man. Cameras flashed and crowds murmured.

"I'm glad you talked me out of wearing high heels," she whispered to him, trying to break the tension that was building inside her.

Alessandro chuckled. "As much as I love to sweep you into my arms, I think we should save that for the bedroom."

At the base of the staircase, they stopped to pose for photographs.

"What's your name?" called a voice from somewhere behind the explosion of flashes.

"This is Ann-Sophie Svensson, my fiancée." Then he bent down and brushed his lips over hers. Before she could recover, he was guiding her up the stairs and into the building, leaving a trail of questions behind them.

In the gallery, signs and ticketing lines had been replaced with flowering plants, red velvet and hundreds of candles. Attendees stood in groups of glittery gowns and black tuxedos. They were entering Alessandro's world, where he was known for relationships that were like fireworks—exciting, explosive and short-lived. Out of the corner of her eye, she saw heads turn once, then again in double takes as they walked in together, the swell of her belly on full display.

Ann-Sophie flashed to that last night in Nice, when

she watched Alessandro walk in with a countess. His world had felt so far away, a bridge that was impossible to cross. And now, so improbably, *she* was the woman walking in with him. All she had to do was get pregnant, she thought wryly, and she was sure more than a few people were thinking the same thing. But then Alessandro looked down at her with the kind of indulgent smile that made her forget about all of that. It took her back into their own private world.

"I ruined your Cinderella moment back in Nice," he whispered in her ear. "But I hope tonight makes up for it."

She raised an eyebrow. "To be determined."

But she couldn't stop herself from smiling. As she reached out to stroke his cheek, she hoped that in her own version of the Cinderella tale, midnight would never come.

Alessandro understood his assignment for tonight. He was to introduce Ann-Sophie into his world and give a display of love that projected the image of a happy couple that their family needed. Tonight was about showing the world that this relationship was not a possible catalyst for going off the rails, as his father's had. And it wouldn't be.

But Ann-Sophie was so beautiful and lovely that Alessandro's chest hurt. And as he walked through the wide hall of the museum, surrounded by relics of art from fallen civilizations, in a place where the present mingled with the past, anything seemed possible.

They walked through the candlelit gallery, past

servers offering flutes of champagne. Not far ahead, the countess caught his eye and gave him a flirtatious smile. It was nothing out of the ordinary, something that she had done countless times. But he was so clearly with another woman—his *pregnant* fiancée—and yet she had felt that it was still appropriate to flirt. As if she was simply waiting her turn before he danced with her. Then again, Alessandro knew that he had given her every reason to expect this. He had conducted himself this way in the past, and never once had he thought twice about it. But the idea that Ann-Sophie could have seen this flirtatious smile, this reminder of what the world expected from him… The unwelcome idea twisted in his stomach.

How had he enjoyed this life before? The question stunned him. Because up until now, he would have said that he had enjoyed his life immensely for all the pleasures it afforded him. And he had taken full advantage of every one of these pleasures. But now, everything about his previous life felt wrong. Empty. The idea of going back to who he was before that day outside Ann-Sophie's apartment building didn't sit well at all with him. So he pushed the thought away and steered them in another direction, toward the dance floor.

"How are we doing so far, Cinderella?" he asked, focusing on the curve of her back under his hand and her lips, the color of ripe peaches.

"I don't think I'll ever get used to a life like this," she said, gesturing to the orchestra and the line of servers, dressed elegantly in black, waiting to attend to the guests. "But I guess you've been doing this forever."

He considered this comment. "It's a role, one I have always played in the family."

"Quite happily, as I remember," she said with a laugh. "You were always flirting, talking with some someone or another, entertaining."

He frowned. "I suppose that's accurate."

"The baby and I are really cramping your lifestyle." She gave him a wry smile.

He didn't smile back. "I haven't been to a single event since Nice."

He hadn't made the decision consciously. He simply hadn't been in the mood, and intuition had always been his best gauge of what to attend, or whom to dance with or whom to sleep with. This was the one place he had allowed himself to be guided by his feelings. And for the last seven months, he simply didn't *want* to be with anyone. He hadn't thought much of it at the time, as he had always had periods where he was busier with more meetings or other obligations, but looking back now, he hadn't had the urge to go out, let alone to sleep with another woman. Since Ann-Sophie. The thought rattled his calm.

Ann-Sophie gave him a skeptical look. "I know you have a past, Alessandro. You didn't know about the baby, and you didn't know you would ever see me again. I wouldn't be at all surprised if you had gone about your life the way you always had."

The string quartet ended the song and there was a pause, a quiet in the room. He should have seen this break as an opening to change course. The most strategic move was to lie and say that he had moved on because the truth—that he had had no interest in other women since their week in Nice—might suggest that he was offering more in their marriage than he was. But honesty was a sore point with her, and though he couldn't give her everything she wanted, he should give her this.

So he looked at her with a seriousness that didn't belong anywhere near this dance floor, with all of society watching them. "I understand that we are allowed to have our pasts. But there has been no one else since you. I promise you that."

Her eyes widened a little, and her breath caught audibly in her throat. The expression that flashed across her face looked too much like hope. Hope she never should have in him. Some part of him wanted to warn her away, but instead, he brought his mouth to hers. He kissed her slowly, teasing her with his lips and the sensual swipe of his tongue, trying to forget that there was a war inside him that had no winners. Trying to convince her that this kiss, this electric connection, could be enough. But soon his own desire turned on him, and he felt his grip of control shake. He pulled away.

She blinked, as if she wasn't quite sure what had just happened. Then she smiled. "Is that your way of ending a discussion?"

"You can take away whatever message you'd like," he said, smiling back, and he felt a bit steadier.

At dinner, he found himself only half paying attention to his conversation with the dewy-eyed heiress he was sitting next to, distracted by the man Ann-Sophie was deep in conversation with across the table. Ernesto Ruzzo, a businessman based in Venice. He was a bit older, good-looking and smiling at Ann-Sophie in a way that was uncomfortably familiar. Especially when his eyes drifted to her generous breasts, so temptingly highlighted by the cut of her dress. Alessandro felt an unfamiliar stab of…jealousy? In the middle of this confusing thought, Ann-Sophie glanced across the table and smiled at him, as if completely unaware of what he was noticing.

That night, as they entered the dark hotel room, he found himself thinking of the man who had been so… attentive.

"Ernesto Ruzzo seemed very taken with you," he said, keeping his voice even as they walked into the living room, lit by the lights that glowed through the French doors.

She shrugged. "We met back in Nice, too, actually."

"He seemed to especially appreciate your dress. Particularly the cut of the neckline." Alessandro complimented himself silently on the way he kept his voice perfectly even.

Ann-Sophie rolled her eyes. "Or maybe he just enjoyed my sparkling conversation."

"Those possibilities are not mutually exclusive," he said darkly.

Tension in his body rose, and for one short moment, he asked himself why he needed to keep up this control. What would happen if he simply let his emotions rule? But he knew the answer. As a teen the results were destructive but not irrevocable. But he was an adult, and with the power and attention he wielded, he could scorch the earth, wreaking havoc on everyone around him. Massimo. The baby. *Ann-Sophie.*

She was studying him, and she sighed. "Fine. I did notice that he might have been distracted by my breasts a few times, but I thought it was harmless because I am quite visibly pregnant with your child right now."

"Men like that might see your situation as an invitation rather than an obstacle."

"Men like that…?" She stopped, as if she was considering a new possibility. "Are you jealous?"

Alessandro shoved away the swell of emotions building inside him and frowned. "Cautious."

That was the most generous word for what he was feeling right now.

"I don't appreciate my behavior being monitored," she said pointedly, and he braced himself for what was next. "But I suppose we both have our demons to struggle with. If we're going to marry, we need to find a way to work together. Support each other."

She gave him a wicked smile that brought him back to one particularly satisfying night in Nice. And then, right there in the living room, she got down on her knees in front of him with a hot burn of desire in her eyes that told him exactly what she meant by *support each other.*

Alessandro knew he should stop her. He knew mixing jealousy and sex was a dangerous game when his control he kept on such a tight leash seemed to be slipping. Yet, he couldn't bring himself to stop it.

"I want to see your breasts." He gritted out the words. "I also find this dress incredibly distracting."

Her wicked smile grew as she slipped the dress off one shoulder, then the other, exposing her generous breasts. He groaned and leaned back against the wall. She turned her attention to his trousers, unfastening them. Then she pulled out his length and licked him, provoking a euphoric shudder so strong his legs shook. She took him in his mouth, and all his tension and jealousy was turning to fire inside him as he watched her pleasure him. Finally, he was allowed to lose control. But he held on to this feeling as long as he could until it was too much, and he came, trembling, leaving him rattled him to the core. He reached down to caress Ann-Sophie's face as he reined in his harsh breaths. Then he lifted her from the ground, and let her to their bed.

"Sit. Please." The words were tight as the need built so precipitously, impossibly fast. She sat on the edge of the bed, and he kneeled in front of her. He moved her panties to the side and found she was warm and so ready for him. So he teased her, letting her gasps spur him until she was crying with pleasure. Then he got to his feet and entered her. He slid in, relishing in how wet she was, how ready she was. She opened her eyes and met his gaze, and he felt a tightness in his chest so strong he had to look away. Instead, he moved, pleasuring her until she arched her back and let herself be washed away is ecstasy. And only after she whimpered and cried out his name did he allow himself to go over the edge again.

CHAPTER NINE

The morning of the wedding, Ann-Sophie sat in her favorite chair in her favorite alcove of the library. A book lay open on her lap, but she was staring out the window at the town below and the narrow road that curved through the olive grove and out of sight. Alessandro had left on that road in the blur of the early morning.

"I have something I must do," he had said vaguely, and she had been too tired to do anything but nod. Now, she wished she had pressed him or said…something. Because today was their wedding day.

He had left like this a handful of times over the last month since she had arrived. And while he had kept his promise to always tell her when he left, with each departure, she had felt acutely aware of how much she didn't know about him. How much he still kept closed off from her. Alessandro had hinted that after the wedding, when he returned to the travel schedule he usually kept, his absences would be more frequent. So she knew the ache of his absence would only grow stronger.

But he wouldn't disappear, she reminded herself, and the baby would not grow up with the ache inside that she had felt, searching for a father that would never be there. A want that had sometimes felt like a need.

Her thoughts were interrupted by the creak of a door and the tap of footsteps on stone. Ann-Sophie's heart took off the way it always seemed to do when she thought of Alessandro. She turned and found not Alessandro, but Massimo's wife walking toward her. Ann-Sophie blinked in surprise. They had not formally met, and yet Massimo and Catarina's relationship had been documented by the paparazzi well enough that Ann-Sophie knew her on sight.

"Ann-Sophie? I'm Catarina." Her voice was enchantingly melodic, and Ann-Sophie was reminded of Catarina's famous mother, the so-called Nordic siren, known for her own captivating voice before her sharp decline into cancer. The loss must weigh heavily on Catarina, Ann-Sophie thought. And suddenly the woman in front of her felt much less like the glamorous and notoriously reclusive heiress that had made a splash in the tabloid not so long ago and more like any other person whose life was subject to the same whims of fate as everyone else.

"I'm glad to finally meet you in person. I'd get up but—" Ann-Sophie gestured to her very present belly. "I'm sorry you arrived when Alessandro isn't here."

"Please don't get up," said Catarina with a laugh and sat in the chair next to her. "I'm here to see you, but I hope I'm not disturbing you."

Ann-Sophie shook her head and set her book on the wooden table next to her. "My mind has been wandering all morning."

Catarina beamed. “Because you’re getting married today.”

Ann-Sophie pushed aside the last of her uneasiness and let herself get carried away by the excitement in Catarina’s voice. Today was her *wedding day.*

“It still feels very unreal. I’m just sitting here in my sundress…” Ann-Sophie gesture to the quiet library.

Catarina gave her a warm smile. “I’ve brought a few things to make this feel more real.”

“I guess I have to get out of this chair someday,” she said with a laugh and began to pry herself out of it.

She followed Catarina through the halls and into a room that looked as if it had once functioned as a sitting room. Now it looked more like backstage at an elegant theater. There was a vanity table set up with a mirror, boxes of makeup and all sorts of tools for hairstyling. Across the room hung the dress that she had chosen back in Rome. It was made by the same designer as the dress she had worn to the museum event, made with the same soft silk, but the neckline was more appropriate for a church. Hanging next to it was a selection of wraps in white silk, and below it more neat stacks of shoeboxes and a flat pink box from a famous lingerie designer. Two women sat on elegantly upholstered chairs by the window, sipping coffee from a service that sat on the table between them. They turned, and their eyes lit with pleasure when they caught sight of Ann-Sophie.

“You are breathtaking,” gushed one of the women as she stood up. She was tall with dark brown eyes and the longest hair Ann-Sophie had ever seen.

"This is Maria, who would love to do your hair for the wedding," said Catarina, then gestured to the petite woman with a sharp black bob. "And this is Elena. She does makeup."

As the women both crossed the room, Catarina added quickly, "No obligation. I just thought it might be fun."

"Definitely," she said, trying to ignore the sudden pang of longing. She should have asked her mother to come. Even if this marriage wasn't for love, it was still a wedding, a celebration. But all of these wants were not needs, she reminded herself. She had enough. In fact, she had so much more than enough. So she pushed the maudlin thoughts out of her head and immersed herself in the extravagant preparations.

The team helped her into her dress, then as she sat down in front of the well-lit vanity, Elena brought out a long black cape to cover her dress. Maria started with her hair, showing pictures of everything from a regal, elegant updo, to a tumble of curls, both of which she promised she could get Ann-Sophie's stick-straight hair to hold.

"My mother used to French-braid my hair in a sort of crown on top of my head," said Ann-Sophie a little wistfully. "Can you do that?"

Maria's eyes lit up. "Absolutely."

The result was a stunning, professional version of her mother's efforts. "Shall I add flowers or something decorative?"

Ann-Sophie flashed to a memory of Midsummer at her grandparents' farm, picking wildflowers with her mother and putting them into each other's hair. "Flowers, please. Small ones."

"I'll help you find some," said Catarina to Maria.

Maria nodded and disappeared through the door with Catarina, and Elena took a seat next to her. She studied Ann-Sophie's face. "You have such a lovely spray of freckles across your nose, and I'd hate to cover them up, especially with this hairstyle. I'm thinking something that works with this and the peach tones of your lips…"

The woman seemed to have a vision for her makeup that Ann-Sophie had never herself had, so she said, "Do what you think will look best."

By the time Maria and Catarina returned, Elena had worked her magic, somehow making Ann-Sophie look like herself, but with a glamorous glow. They drank coffee and ate from a tray of fruit and pastries that Olivia dropped off. Maria wove flowers into her hair and Catarina fussed over her shoes—

"No heels," said Maria and Elena in unison when Ann-Sophie teetered on a particularly high pair—and then, with a flare of drama, Elena pulled off the protective cape, revealing her full look.

Ann-Sophie stood in front of the mirror, gazing at herself in wonder. Catarina came up next to her and held out a large jewelry box, tied with a dark blue ribbon.

"Alessandro wanted to give this to you himself, but I chased him away," she said. Ann-Sophie's heart took off in her chest—Alessandro had returned. "I want him to be surprised by all this."

She gestured to the dress and her hair, and Ann-Sophie felt a surge of warmth toward this woman whom she had just met but had made her wedding day a little more special. Ann-Sophie untied the ribbon and opened the old-fashioned box. On top of it was a note, just three words written on thick creamy paper with the words *For my wife*. Nothing more. How strange that her chest seem to expand with the simple words. She had never seen his handwriting before. How fitting, she thought, as she traced the messy scrawl with her fingers before she remembered that she wasn't alone. Ann-Sophie lifted the note and looked inside. Nestled in the silk was a necklace with sapphires and diamonds hanging from it. The pendant earrings were echoes of the same jeweled pattern.

"Oh," she whispered, not knowing what else to say.

"I'm pretty sure these belong to his grandmother," said Catarina. "Do you want to try them on?"

She nodded, and Catarina reached around and fastened the clasp. Ann-Sophie gazed in the mirror one more time. Was this really her life? It seemed so improbable.

The limo waited outside, and she and Catarina rode through the village streets into the palazzo, where the church loomed like an elegant warning. If the Carandini villa was a monument to the eras that had passed, a mishmash of stone and bricks gathered and replaced overtime, the church was the opposite, preserved firmly in the past, as if it had not needed repairs to combat centuries of decay. As if it was preserved by the will of God alone. Catarina helped her out of the car and together they walked across the cobblestone path and through the heavy wooden door.

It took a moment for Ann-Sophie's eyes to adjust. All she could see was the glow of candles everywhere. But after a moment, Alessandro came into focus. He stood by the altar in a tuxedo that hugged his broad shoulders and emphasized his considerable height. And he was looking at her with an intensity that took her breath away. She and Catarina started down the aisle, and as they walked, the priest and Massimo and the exquisite relics from the past all faded away. There was just Alessandro and the thump of her heart, so full of want and hope. Today, she was marrying him. She told herself that this feeling was enough. Tomorrow, she could worry about everything else.

When she reached the altar, Alessandro's mouth lifted in a smile so warm and intimate that her heart jumped in her chest. "You look beautiful."

The ceremony was like a dream, with Alessandro's warm, large hand the only thing tethering her to reality. When it was time to recite their vows, she found that promises of love fell from her lips like drops of truth she wondered if he could hear. And when he spoke the words of love, she let herself hope that he meant the kind of love that came with time and closeness, not duty. Just for today she could hope, she told herself, because he was looking at her with brown eyes, so dark and solemn that she wondered if he was thinking the same. And when he kissed her, his lips lingered on hers, and under the ever-present heat, she felt something stir between them, something she could believe in. Just for today.

* * *

Alessandro sat at the long table, lit by candles, gazing at his wife. *His wife.* Every time that thought ran through his head, it made the tenuous armor of his control crack, breaking too fast for him to repair. And yet he couldn't stop himself from repeating these words, over and over. *His wife.*

He should return to Milan tonight and get control of himself, the way he had every time in the last month that the intensity of being near her had gotten too strong. They were married. His task had been accomplished. And yet he could not make himself leave. Even this morning, leaving her for a few hours had not sat well, even when it was to drive to his grandmother's house so Ann-Sophie could have pieces of the Carandini family jewelry.

Alessandro had counted on her mother's arrival as a distraction that would ease the sting of his departure. He had arranged for Margarita Svensson to fly on a private jet, timed perfectly for the morning of their wedding, and yet, she had not shown up. It had shaken him, despite the fact that Ann-Sophie knew nothing about this plan. He, too, had not expected his own parents' presence, despite the fact that Masimo had mentioned the wedding to them the week before. Both he and Ann-Sophie had been forged by these parental relationships, and they would serve as guide on what *not* to do, he told himself. He was also counting on this to mean that Ann-Sophie would accept the limits in their own relationship because he would not abandon the child.

But those moments in the church today had not just been about the child. He had felt something stir inside him as he looked into the endless rivers of her eyes and spoke his promises of love. For a few, beautiful moments at the altar, as his end goal played out, he found he was not thinking of goals or next steps or any of the tactics he used to keep himself in safe territory. It was hard to make sense of what had happened there, as he spoke his vows. Everything that drove him seemed to fade, and it was only Ann-Sophie.

Now, as he sat in the formal dining room of the villa, lit by candles, he knew he should take this as a warning sign. He knew he had to leave. And he would.

After the night was over.

Alessandro focused on Ann-Sophie as she talked with Catarina and Massimo, so comfortably, and something about that made the turmoil inside grow stronger.

So he rose to his feet and looked from Catarina to Massimo. "We'll see you in the morning."

Ann-Sophie's cheeks turned a delightful pink, and she glanced at Alessandro, then back at his brother and his wife. "Please excuse this man's manners. I don't know where he got his reputation for being a smooth talker."

Massimo let out a little bark of laughter. "I couldn't have said it better myself."

Ann-Sophie's amused smile turned hotter as they started through the halls and climbed the ancient stairs. But instead of leading her to the bedroom they had shared, he turned down a different hall and led her to the very end of it. When he opened the door, he felt a surge of satisfaction at the catch of her breath as Ann-Sophie took in their surroundings.

The room was much larger than the one they had stayed in. It was the master suite that his grandparents had occupied for a time before they gave the villa over to his parents, and it was covered with flowers. Olivia and Cinzia had spent the morning gathering tangles of rambling rose in white and every shade of pink, and the room sighed with the heavy scent. The flowering vines hung from the tall windows and twined around the balcony. The French doors were open, letting the warm breeze blow new life into this place, pushing out the ghosts of the past. Bouquets of wildflowers from the hillside sat on the bureaus and tables, and the room was bathed in the glow of the sunset.

Alessandro didn't speak. He simply led her along a path of rose petals to the enormous bed, covered in a billowy cloud-like duvet. A sudden rush of joy overtook him as Ann-Sophie stood in front of him. *His wife.* Her smile was warm and intimate, and he ached with a desire that he didn't fully understand, and a thought ran through his head, one he realized had been building inside him. Maybe this could work. Maybe he could change. Maybe she and the baby would change him and these emotions that bubbled inside him would no longer lead to anger and destruction. He let the temptation of these thoughts guide each touch.

Slowly, he undressed her, memorizing the way it felt to run his hands up her growing belly as he lifted the dress, tracing the fullness of her breasts and the dip of her collarbone. He kissed every one of these places, closing his eyes and memorizing them with his lips. When he finished, she lifted his hand from his own shirt, silently insisting that she undress him, too. She removed his cuff links, studying his hands, and unfastened each button on his shirt. His muscles tensed as her hands explored. Her blue eyes were focused, as if she was discovering something new. It all felt new, as if she was uncovering the layers he kept between himself and the world. Suddenly he was being exposed, and yet, he didn't stop her. He gritted his teeth against each flash of desire and let her take her time until they both stood naked, facing each other. He traced a line up her arm, over her shoulders and up her slim neck until he was cupping her jaw. And then he kissed her.

His body was on fire and his instincts told him to bring them to the ecstasy they both craved, but he held back, just kissing her with the aching desire mixed with something else he wasn't going to contemplate. Her hands explored his body, a whisper over the planes of his chest and the ridges of his abs, until it was too much. Wordlessly, he pulled back. And they stood there for a moment, gazes matched, until that became a different kind of too much. So he led her to the bed and he fixed the pillows so she was comfortable. And then he kneeled before her and entered her. Her eyes met his as she let out a gasp, and he clenched his teeth against the insatiable need to lose himself in the pleasure, in this one place he allowed himself total abandon.

But tonight she held his gaze, and tonight he couldn't look away. Slowly, he began to move, tilting his hips, finding the angle that made her gasp, then luxuriating in that angle with hard, long thrusts. Still, her gaze was on his, open and vulnerable, and he had no idea what she saw in his, but she didn't look away. The pleasure between them grew until she gasped and moaned and fell over the edge of bliss. As he followed her, he could have sworn that he saw tears well in her eyes before she closed them, and it felt as if something had torn inside of him, something that felt ominously irreparable.

He lay beside her in silence in the aftermath, touching. She stroked his cheek and ran her hand over his biceps, and he flexed his muscles playfully, teasing out a smile from her. They hadn't spoken a word, and yet it felt as if he had somehow bared his soul to her and she had done the same. And neither of them had looked away.

He had no idea when they drifted off to sleep, but sometime in the early morning, Alessandro started awake. He sat up in bed, looking for whatever had startled him. An uneasy feeling washed over him, and yet when he looked next to him, there was Ann-Sophie with a sleepy smile. A flicker of relief cut through the unease, but as he bent down to kiss her, a voice floated through the open window, so sickeningly familiar. It cut through all the hopes that had run through his mind and exposed them for the lie they were. Nothing would change.

CHAPTER TEN

"OLIVIA. I NEED you at once. I simply cannot handle all this baggage alone…"

The voice coming through the open French doors sounded irritated, as if the woman speaking was unaware of the exasperated tone she was using at—Ann-Sophie checked the stately clock that ticked on the wall—6:14 a.m.?

"I apologize, *Signora*—"

Before Olivia's voice had reached the end of the last word, the other woman's voice began again. "Travel has been a complete nightmare. The storms ruined the last three days in Seychelles, and then, the pilot had the nerve to tell us that he would not fly in the weather. Can you imagine? So I asked him what we were paying him for. Why were we paying the salary of a pilot who won't fly? I demanded the very moment that the airport would allow that we would leave. Which happened to be late at night. As you can imagine, sleeping on the plane, no matter how comfortable they say the beds are on planes, they just never lit live up to expectations. And then…"

The words were now muffled in the distance, leaving only hints of that distinctive voice. Ann-Sophie rubbed her eyes and tried to get her thoughts in order. She opened her mouth to ask Alessandro what was going on, but when she turned to him, his expression had gone blank. The only hint of emotion was an ominous tightness in his jaw.

His mother. It had to be her. Just her voice had taken every ounce of softness, every hint of raw vulnerability that she had seen in him the night before, and turned it all to stone. She lifted her hand to his face, but he flinched and moved away.

"My parents have arrived, only a day late for the wedding." His voice was hard. "I should introduce you."

He managed to make this sound like a threat. Ann-Sophie told herself that this was painful for him, but the past night he had opened himself to her. They could get through this. So she got dressed and brushed her hair. When they started down the staircase, the hand he offered her felt like the one he had offered on the walk home from the doctor's clinic, out of duty rather than care. Ever the gentleman, she thought darkly.

They walked through the endless halls, following that voice and its endless string of commentary and complaints. Ann-Sophie felt as if they were walking to their execution. The thought was a bit dramatic, but when she glanced at Alessandro and squeezed his hand, searching for their connection, he didn't look at her. Instead, he released her hand and continued into the dining room, where Olivia and Cinzia were bringing platters of food to the table.

"Good morning," said Olivia, giving Alessandro what looked like a worried glance. But Alessandro didn't seem to notice. He was looking at his parents.

His mother was, in the most objective sense, lovely, a combination of nature and money that made the most of her features. She wore a cream silk blouse and matching wool trousers that accentuated her fashionably thin figure, and her hair was twisted in a neat updo that suggested careful preparation rather than a night of hardship. She was talking to Alessandro's father, who was reading the newspaper and murmuring in agreement. Neither of his parents seemed to notice their entry until they stood next to the table.

His mother's gaze lifted to her son with a flicker of disappointment. "Alessandro, where is your brother? We were told he was here. We need to talk to him about our flat in Milan, which was simply not usable when we arrived, after hours of horrendous travel."

Alessandro's jaw tightened. "Mother, Father, I would like you to meet my wife, Ann-Sophie."

His father looked up over his newspaper, and gave Ann-Sophie a brusque once-over, then turned back to his newspaper. His mother's gaze was more assessing, and she furrowed her brow, as if confused. Her eyes traveled down Ann-Sophie's body, stopping at her very prominent belly. Then she looked back at Alessandro and gave him an exasperated smile. "Oh, yes. I do remember Massimo mentioning something about a wedding to someone, but it was too…" She waved her hand as if the excuse was self-explanatory. Then her gaze sharpened as it settled on her belly. "Now, I understand."

Ann-Sophie stared at this woman, who had no memory of her son's wedding and certainly no intention of coming for it. She seemed to exist on an entirely different plane of reality—one where everything centered on her.

His mother still hadn't stopped talking. "Poor girl. You got knocked up by the wrong brother. But I suppose he does come with money, so he has some appeal."

Ann-Sophie froze, so horrified by the casual cruelty this woman—Alessandro's *mother*—was capable of. Alessandro had told her, but she hadn't expected…this.

"Get. Out." Alessandro's voice was low and cold enough to make his father look up from his paper.

"You have no right to tell us to get out of our home," his mother said dismissively. Then she turned back to the coffee in front of her and busied herself with the creamer.

"*Get out of this house.*" This time, Alessandro's voice was louder. Harder. Ann-Sophie found herself trembling, not for herself but for Alessandro. All at once, she felt the surge of anger that he kept so carefully buried. This was the emotion he feared, and she was watching as it began to consume him. She had no idea what to do. There was so much hurt behind this and she felt a helplessness that made her angry, too. No one should have to endure the kind of callousness that Alessandro had come to expect from his mother.

"Son." His father put down the paper, and his voice was filled with warning.

"This is not your house," Alessandro snapped at his father. "It hasn't been since you drove your father's business into the ground."

"That might be true," said his mother coldly, as if she was not watching her son's anguish play out in front of her. "But, since you insist on specifics, we all know it's Massimo who keeps this family's fortunes afloat, not you. We'll leave this decision up to him."

Fury blazed from Alessandro's eyes. Ann-Sophie reached for his hand, but he yanked it away.

"Don't." The words came out as cold and hard as the look he gave her. It was the same one he had given his parents. Something twisted in her stomach. She wrapped her hands around her belly protectively, as if shielding the baby from his glare.

"Please, Alessandro," she whispered, fighting every instinct to leave this place, run far away. "Go upstairs. I will meet you there."

He looked at her, but it was as if he didn't quite see her, his gaze was so full of anger. It was as if he was unraveling right in front of her eyes.

"No. You need to get far away from here," he snapped. "And don't come back."

It was an arrow straight for her heart, and it hit. Ann-Sophie startled at the intensity of his voice. Anger and anguish seemed to ricochet between them. Everything about this hurt.

Alessandro closed his eyes. Ran a hand through his hair.

"*Go*," he said, biting out the word.

Ann-Sophie swallowed, torn between his plea and

her instinct not to leave him alone with his parents. He glared at her, or maybe it was a plea. It didn't matter. She took a step back. Another. And another until she was at the threshold of the hallway.

When she rounded the corner, out of sight, Alessandro's voice boomed, "If you don't leave my house, I will physically remove you."

It was as if the entire house went still, and in the silence, Ann-Sophie understood that the threat was not empty. Tension coiled around her, and she stopped in her tracks as her belly seized. *Deep, calming breaths.* She took a shaky approximation of a yoga breath and reminded herself that she had four more weeks before the baby was due. Even the false contractions made it sometimes feel like it would be sooner. Ann-Sophie stood frozen in the hallway, trying to breathe her way out of this mess, until the scrape of a chair on the tile floor released her.

Footsteps.

Ann-Sophie started down the hallway, away from the dining room, but her belly seized again. She headed for an armchair and sank into the red velvet cushion.

Deep, calming breaths.

The footsteps grew louder, and when she looked up, Alessandro's mother was there.

"I'm sure this display was educational," the woman said with a forced lightness, but the high flush in her cheeks suggested she was unsettled. "He's always been like that."

As if Alessandro was a teenager throwing a temper tantrum. As if his mother hadn't noticed any other part of him for more than half of his life. Because this description of Alessandro had absolutely no basis in the man that she knew. It was a portrait of the teenage boy Alessandro had hinted at, one he had worked to leave behind. One that haunted him for very real reasons, she reminded herself.

His father came up behind his mother but kept his gaze fixed on the front door.

"I am carrying your grandchild," said Ann-Sophie quietly. "Nothing is more important to me than protecting my family from the kind of harm you so clearly have given Alessandro for his whole life."

His mother turned away, but Ann-Sophie continued. "You have been trading on the Carandini name for years, as far as I can tell, so let me make this clear. If you ever speak to any of us like this again, I will make sure the press knows exactly why we won't allow you around your grandchild."

His father's gaze landed firmly on her, and she got the sense that he was seeing her for the first time. He paused, his eyes narrowed, before he looked away and continued to the door. As the heavy wooden door shut behind Alessandro's parents, Ann-Sophie promised herself that she would do everything in her power to protect her child, no matter where that took her.

Alessandro paced across the dining room like a caged animal. But no matter how many times he stalked back and forth, the anger inside him would not go away. His mother's careless cruelty hadn't just been aimed at him. It had been aimed straight for Ann-Sophie, too, and that had pushed him over the edge. He had not only brought another innocent person into the mess of his family, but he had also let his anger flare out of control. Enough that he had lashed out at Ann-Sophie.

Alessandro glared at the room around him. The excess of food and elegant dishware, combined with the heady scent of the flowers from their wedding, all seemed to mock him with the naive illusion of the night before, when he let himself wonder if he had finally escaped the wounds of his childhood. How wrong he had been. How quickly their poisoned legacy had found him.

Better now than after the baby was born, he thought darkly.

He didn't hear Ann-Sophie enter. He didn't notice her until she was standing right in front of him. The look of devastation on her face dissolved any control he'd managed to claw back. He was so fucking angry at all of this mess.

"I warned you," he said, gritting out the words through clenched teeth. "All along, I warned you."

"They're awful," she said quietly. "I'm so sorry you—"

"*Don't*," he growled, cutting her off. "You know nothing about me."

But the sharpness of his words was like a punch in his own gut. He stumbled back to a chair and sank down in it, his elbows on his knees, his hands buried in his hair.

"I'm leaving," he added when his voice was a little more under control.

The room was quiet, and then her voice came, quiet but determined. “I’ll come with you.”

“You are the last thing I need right now,” he groaned. The words came before he could think to hold them back, and the cruelty of the statement hit him again in his gut. Ever his mother’s son.

But being near Ann-Sophie was simply too much right now. She made him *feel*. Even pleasure, the one place he had allowed himself to follow his instincts, was tainted with every other emotion. She had stripped away the barrier he had built and left him vulnerable at the worst possible moment. It occurred to him that this had been his fear for some time now—that he was hurting Ann-Sophie and he was continuing to hurt her, ruining every ounce of good they had found between them.

Alessandro needed to be far away from her, to close this open wound and get himself under control the way he had all those years ago, after their last expulsion from school. Leaving would hurt Ann-Sophie, but not worse than staying. How could she not see this? Alessandro took a deep breath as grim determination edged out a little of his anger. But when he looked up, Ann-Sophie was clutching her belly, and the anger and sadness had faded from her expression. Instead, he saw pain.

Alessandro shot up from his chair. “What’s happening?”

Ann-Sophie met his gaze, and her eyes were filled with fear. “It’s the baby. Something’s wrong.”

CHAPTER ELEVEN

THE ROAD TO the village was much rougher than Ann-Sophie remembered it. Or maybe it was just that every single bump seemed to trigger another pain in her belly. Still a month before delivery, she told herself, but her worries were growing. Which certainly were not helping her blood pressure. The doctor had warned of so-called false contractions, but Ann-Sophie was pretty sure they weren't supposed to feel like this. Her baby was telling her something, and it couldn't be anything good.

"Tell me what is happening." Alessandro's voice broke through her worries. "Has anything changed?"

His mouth was a grim line of determination as he drove the car along the narrow road that led to the village. In her mind, she flashed to the stark terror on his face when he looked up and saw her in pain. All of his anger and frustration disappeared, and she was almost sure she saw... *Think about that later*, she told herself, pushing the memory away.

"Nothing's changed. It's just..." She groaned as the pain hit her again, shooting across her back. She took a couple of deep breaths, then tried again. "It's like my entire belly is seizing up. And that covers quite a lot of me these days."

"Just a few more minutes and we're there," he said. "The doctor will be waiting for us."

"Never have I hated cobblestones so much in my life," she muttered.

The car screeched to a stop in front of the clinic, and Alessandro rushed around to help her out of the car. The doctor and three other staff members came to the door and helped her into the bed that was waiting for her. One attendant wheeled her into the room as another took her vitals, then began to hook her up to a series of monitors. Her heartbeat skittered across the screen, ticking higher as her belly seized again.

Just as the pain was taking hold, Alessandro slipped his hand into hers. "Squeeze my hand and take a deep breath."

Ann-Sophie gave him a bewildered look. Just moments ago, he was walking out the door, and now…

She cried out and squeezed as hard as she could.

"Good job," he said, brushing her hair from her face. "Just keep breathing."

"What if something happens to the baby?" she pleaded, gasping for breath.

"Nothing bad will happen." Alessandro's voice was tight.

"We don't know that." Tears began to well, but she fought against them.

His brown eyes were dark and so intense, and she saw fear leaking into his gaze, a fear that mirrored her own. "We don't."

"It's not supposed to go like this," she whispered.

"I want to make this better for you. For the baby. And I can't." His voice broke, and he swallowed, his Adam's apple bobbing in his throat. "But I will be here for you. We're in this together."

Dr. Cantabella looked up from the fetal heartbeat screen and said, "The baby is coming today."

Ann-Sophie stared at the doctor. "I… I'm not due for another month."

The doctor frowned. "Babies have a mind of their own when it comes to due dates. I suppose it's to get to prepare us for life as parents."

"But it's too early," she protested weakly. This was feeling all too much like the visit to the doctor back in Stockholm, the last time her body demanded something she was not ready for.

The doctor nodded. "It is early, but we will meet whatever needs your baby has."

Before Ann-Sophie had a chance to fully process this news, another contraction—because that was what this pain was—hit her.

She sucked in a sharp breath, and Alessandro tensed.

"Can something be done for all her pain?" he growled. "This can't be right. She's suffering."

"We have pain-mitigation options," said the woman gently. "But some partners find it easier to wait elsewhere while the baby comes."

He frowned and shook his head. "If she has to go through this, I will be here."

Alessandro Carandini was a man of his word. He stayed by her through every minute of it, coaching her breaths and stroking her forehead. In the back of her mind, she was still hurt and frustrated, but those feelings faded because the baby was coming. Quickly, in fact. It was all a blur of pain and brusque voices until, finally, the doctor handed her their baby boy. A beautiful baby with wisps of dark hair and bronze skin so much like his father's. Alessandro kneeled by her side as the tiny baby let out a wail.

"He takes after me," he said with a hint of dark humor, but his eyes were filled with astonishment.

It felt as if her heart was expanding in her chest as she looked from Alessandro to this tiny, beautiful baby. A halo of love was growing around her, pushing out their disastrous start to the morning and filling her with joy.

"Hello, little one," she whispered. "Welcome."

The doctor slipped an oxygen mask over the baby's tiny head and pressed a heart monitor to his chest. "We need to do some testing, but this little guy looks strong, so we will give your family a few moments first."

And then, they were alone. The baby's eyes closed, and she wondered at the fact that this moment she had both worried about and dreamed about for so long was finally here. They had a *baby*, the tiniest, most joyful person she had ever seen.

"We will meet whatever needs you have, my love," she whispered to him, as the truth of Dr. Cantabella's words echoed inside her.

Alessandro hadn't said a word, and his expression was inscrutable.

"Can I hold him?" he asked softly.

Ann-Sophie lifted the baby in his arms and held him close, his big, scarred hands cradling the tiny body, and he whispered in a low voice. Tears welled in her eyes as every strong emotion cascaded at once. This day had been filled with so much grief and so much joy, it seemed impossibly overwhelming.

Alessandro's face was etched with a kind of wonder, but as he handed the baby back to her, the expression faded, shifting to something she couldn't read. "I will go back to the villa and pick up anything you need. Then, when you are ready, I will leave for Milan."

She blinked. "When I'm ready?"

"I promised I wouldn't leave you, and I will respect that promise. You're with a newborn, our child." His voice wavered with a hint of emotion, but when he spoke again, it was gone. "I will not abandon you or the child. But I think it's clear that this situation is untenable."

"What situation?" she asked slowly, and the halo of warmth and joy that had surrounded her just moments before was shifting into something that felt much more ominous.

"*This.*" He gestured to the three of them, this tentative little family she couldn't stop herself from wanting. "This has already gone too far. I let out enough poison to send you into early labor. This could've ended so much worse."

He swiped a hand over his face, and she almost missed the haunted look in his eyes.

She let out an exasperated huff. "I know your power

in the world is great, but you do not reign over my body."

Alessandro managed to look both doubtful and smug, and Ann-Sophie felt a flash of something more complicated than desire, adding more fuel to the cauldron of her emotions.

"Your parents are callous and cruel," she continued, "and as far as I can tell, you've been bottling up your very understandable anger for over a decade, pretending that nothing touches you. Or maybe you even started to believe it." She ignored his frown and continued. "Of course, it's going to be messy when it comes out. The real question is what you will choose to do now."

"I'm doing what's best for all three of us," he said, frustration seeping into his voice.

"You're doing what's easiest instead of fighting for what we could have," she snapped. Ann-Sophie regretted her words even before his expression shuttered. Desperation was starting to take hold inside her.

"I love you," she insisted. "Not some public image of you but the man I have spent the past month with. That's why I married you. Not just for the baby. I know I was not supposed to fall in love with you, but I have."

And as she spoke the words, she felt the depth of truth behind them. She had told herself marriage was best for the baby, but she knew better than anyone that it was love, not marriage, that made the biggest difference for a child. Alessandro's parents were a stark reminder.

His expression was hard and cold. "You know I cannot give you what you're asking me for. I was clear from the beginning."

She had not asked him for love, not directly, but he had heard it, anyway. But this was a want, not a need, she told herself. Even if it did not feel that way. Even if it felt like something inside her was breaking.

"That is your final decision?" she asked softly.

"It is not a decision. It is our reality."

Ann-Sophie swallowed and forced herself to do what was right. For all three of them.

"Then I absolve you of your promise. I am not afraid of raising a child on my own. Of being on my own." Her voice was so much stronger than she felt. "I will never keep you away from your son—it will be too hard for us to spend time together if you refuse to let yourself free of the grip that the past has on you. So whatever we had between us has to end. I don't want to see you, at least until this is less painful."

He flinched, as if she had slapped him. "You knew I had to offer. You accepted that."

"It's not enough." The word *enough* felt strange as she spoke it, as if it was growing, taking on new meaning.

Alessandro was watching her, his beauty made harsh with the pain that radiated from him. Slowly, Alessandro lifted his hands, palms open, as if he was offering himself to her. His expression was stark. "Am I not enough?"

Ann-Sophie froze as the word *enough* twisted yet again inside her, its sharpest edge finding its way straight to her own wound, the one that had never gone away. Alessandro's question was so raw, so full of honesty. So full of the same unhealed hurt she had been running from. He wasn't hiding it anymore, and somehow it made the devastation of his decision even worse.

"You *are* enough," she said as desperation spread its tendrils through her. "I saw what happened when your parents provoked you, and I'm not scared. I want to be there for you, the way you were there for me through this birth. But you're pushing me away when we both need more. We can be so much more for each other. You *have* to know that."

He lowered his hands but said nothing. She searched his expression for some sign that her message was getting through to him, but all she found was a haunted emptiness in his eyes. And in that moment, she could feel the future of the path they were on taking shape. They would break each other's hearts, over and over again, if she compromised.

Ann-Sophie swallowed, trying to ignore the lump in her throat. "I can't do this halfway. If you cannot commit to this—to us—then everything between us is over."

He kissed the baby on the forehead and stroked his cheek with a gentleness that took her breath away, and then he walked out the door.

Alessandro stormed through the front door of the villa, determined not to let his unruly emotions get the better of him for the second time today. He was angry at himself. He was frustrated with Ann-Sophie for stubbornly refusing to understand the reality of their situation. And he was overwhelmed by this tide of fear and intimacy and joy that had flowed at the birth of his son and then seemed to drain from him the moment he had walked away. But he had no other choice.

Alessandro gritted his teeth and reined in that out-of-control feeling inside him. He *would not* lash out again. This was straight out of his mother's playbook, and he would not be like his mother. Not at any price. How could Ann-Sophie be sympathetic after the cruelty that had slipped out of his mouth before he had gotten a chance to think better of it? He didn't deserve sympathy. He had failed himself and he had failed to protect her. And yet, she told him that she loved him.

"Hormones," he muttered to himself as he walked up the stairs.

Yet she had looked at him with a seriousness that he couldn't dismiss so easily. Maybe he should send Catarina to bring her belongings, as she and Ann-Sophie seemed to have bonded at the wedding. Or maybe he should call her mother again. Because if he saw Ann-Sophie and the baby again when he was so wracked with…emotions, he wouldn't be able to leave.

Alessandro reached the top of the familiar staircase and turned toward the master bedroom, where he and Ann-Sophie had spent one magical night together. Until his parents spread their poison through the house. Alessandro frowned. His stomach clenched as he thought of their tiny baby, so helpless. Alessandro had wanted to take that baby and run as far away from his parents as he could get. But that was the heart of the problem, wasn't it? He had been running for his entire adult life, and he still could not escape his parents, not when they were so deeply embedded in him. It was why he had to separate himself from Ann-Sophie and the baby.

But he refused to play that last heartbreaking scene over in his head again, so instead he focused on the tasks in front of him. But as he turned the corner, toward the master bedroom, he came to a stop at an open door. The door to his own childhood bedroom.

He stood at the threshold and peered inside it. Who had been in there? Certainly not his parents. They had rarely entered the room, even when he slept there as a child. He stepped inside, this forgotten relic of his past. On the walls were posters of football greats, now long-retired, and on the bookshelf was a collection of cars of all sizes, hiding the few books, their spines unbroken, given to him before the family had given up on his reading.

He had avoided this room, not wanting to go back to the time when his parents had so much more influence on his life. But as he wandered inside, a different set of memories floated through his mind. They transported him back to a time when he felt a strange kind of peace. A time before he was always angry at his parents, back when he was glad when they would disappear and leave him and Massimo with Olivia and her sister, Natalia, who were so good at allowing the twins to simply be themselves. They swam and kicked the football and wandered into the town for bakery treats, climbing scraggly olive trees along the way. Alessandro hadn't come back here, not wanting to kick the hornet's nest of childhood memories, but as he looked around, he remembered a kind of freedom. A time when his negligent parents had not steered his life.

The real question is what you will choose to do now. Ann-Sophie's voice came back to him, as if she had been there, next to him all along. Alessandro heard footsteps in the hallway and turned, hoping that somehow she would appear. But it wasn't Ann-Sophie that walked into his bedroom. It was Massimo.

His brother raised his eyebrows. "I saw you and Ann-Sophie leave, and she was clutching her belly. What's going on?"

The question shook him back to the present. "She had the baby. A boy."

Massimo frowned. "Is everything okay?"

Not remotely. But he said, "They are both healthy."

His brother looked at him with a gaze sharp enough to make Alessandro look away.

"Why are you in my old room?"

The corners of Massimo's mouth quirked up. "I was telling Catarina about that time I spent a good six months sleeping in this room."

Alessandro hadn't thought about that in a long, long time. "I forgot about your nightmares."

Massimo had awoken, night after night, crying inconsolably, until Olivia had finally moved a second bed into Alessandro's room to see if it would help. It worked so well that Massimo stayed there for months, until Olivia had found them awake at four in the morning, building an enormous racetrack for their cars on a school night. Massimo had returned to his bedroom, and they had all moved on. His brother was such a stoic, determined man that Alessandro, who didn't make a habit of thinking about the past, had allowed incidents like these to fade away.

"Why aren't you with the baby and Ann-Sophie?" His brother was as irritatingly direct as he was persistent.

"We do not have the kind of relationship that warrants my presence. Now that the baby is here, she will likely go back to Stockholm. I will visit them, to make sure I'm a part of the child's life, of course." He delivered this all in a matter-of-fact tone that only confirmed his decision. His voice was under control, even if it felt as if a knife twisted in his gut each time he thought of them.

His brother's eyes narrowed. "I heard every word between you and our parents this morning. I am pretty sure the entire household did."

"Then you must have heard the way I lashed out at Ann-Sophie, too." That knife twisted again, cutting deeper. "I was angry and the words just came out. At her."

He closed his eyes. Even saying this was painful.

"I had forgotten how awful Mother could be to you," said Massimo softly. "I think I just blocked it out, but when I heard her, it all came back."

"Poor little rich kid," he said, trying to lighten the mood a little.

Massimo didn't bite. "I should not have agreed to tell them about the wedding."

"They didn't come for it," he said, his voice filled

with bitterness. "Their appearance was just a happy coincidence."

His brother shook his head. "They shouldn't be in our lives. At all."

"It's okay. I've solved the problem."

Massimo frowned. "What do you mean?"

"Ann-Sophie and I are over. Their poison won't reach her and the baby, and neither will mine."

"What?"

Alessandro glared at his brother, who was making this conversation more painful than it had to be, but Massimo just glared back.

"It's better if I disengage," he said with a finality that marked the end of the topic.

Massimo ignored it. "I heard what she said to our parents. She was fighting for *you*."

"I can't give her what she wants," he said, biting out the words. "It's that simple, so drop it."

His brother, of course, ignored him.

"Has she told you she loves you?" Massimo said it in that voice that suggested already he knew the answer.

"It was the hormones talking," he grumbled.

Massimo let out a huff of laughter. "Even I know not to say that to a woman."

Alessandro scrubbed his face with his hands. "I didn't say it."

"But you wrote off her words just the same." His brother's voice was more serious.

That was true, but why was Massimo being so obtuse about this? Alessandro took a deep breath and laid out the unvarnished reality. "I know our parents are negligent and our mother says things that should never come out of anyone's mouth, but let's not pretend that her words are not based in the truth. I *was* the problem child. I *did* create havoc in this house and drove them away. We both know I would have failed out of school without a little help from money, and I still got us kicked out three times for fights I dragged you into. The last time I almost took you down with me." Alessandro shook his head slowly. "If we hadn't gotten another chance after that, I would have never forgiven myself. I have devoted my life to getting our family's business back for you because I will not let you down again. But a family life? That's not in the cards for me."

His brother was looking at him with an expression that looked very close to stunned. In fact, Alessandro could not remember a time when he had seen his brother looks so surprised.

"Alessandro, it's true that I am very dedicated to our family business. But do you know why I threw myself into it? It was for us. So we wouldn't get pulled in opposite directions. So we could be on a path together." He frowned. "Why do you think I jumped into all those fights with you back at school? Half the time you deserved to get beaten up. But I don't think you ever thought a step further than that fight. What would happen if you walked down to the headmaster's office alone? Our parents would have split us up in a minute. They wouldn't have thought twice before sending you to another school far away. You are my family, and getting split up from you was my personal idea of hell."

The words shook him. Alessandro never considered the larger possible consequences of his fights. It never occurred to him that they could be split up, though now it seemed so obvious. And life without his brother would have been untenable. Unthinkable.

The same way that leaving Ann-Sophie and the baby felt right now.

He pushed that thought away and shook his head. “The moment I go off the rails, I’m going to bring someone down that I love—”

He cut himself off as the echo of his own words rattled through him. He *loved* them. Not just the tiny, beautiful baby, so fragile he was afraid to hold him. He loved Ann-Sophie. And he was afraid he was going to destroy that love.

His brother raised his eyebrows, as if he could read all of Alessandro’s thoughts. Then he ran his hand through his hair.

“If it wasn’t your temper, it would have been something else,” said Massimo, his voice harder. “Mother needed an excuse. She *couldn’t* care about us, and she was always searching for ways to blame us. It might have been my nightmares if Olivia hadn’t hidden them from our parents—because she knew it would make me a target.” He expression softened. “I’m sorry it was you. If I had understood any of this at the time, I would have defended you.”

A strange heaviness washed over Alessandro as Massimo’s words sank in. It felt as if his anger was draining out of his body, leaving what had lay underneath it the entire time: The heavy sadness that their parents had found every excuse to blame the boys for the fact that they just didn't care very much. Alessandro had done everything not to see this most obvious truth.

The room was silent. Finally, Alessandro gave a rough laugh. "Have you been googling *traumatic childhood* again?"

Massimo smirked. "Catarina drags this kind of thing out of me. Something about emotional openness."

Alessandro and Massimo scoffed in unison, the way they had so many times when they were younger, but Alessandro could see that Massimo wasn't one bit unhappy about his situation.

"If your temper was incompatible with caring for someone, I would have left you behind at one of those schools long ago," he said pointedly, then raised an eyebrow. "I saw Ann-Sophie's necklace at the wedding. I assume you went to see our grandmother. What did she say to you?"

Alessandro shrugged. "Some nonsense about being so in love that I forgot to invite her to the wedding."

"When I was there for the ring, she said that I had spent my life defying our parents in every area. Why wouldn't I do it for love?"

Alessandro gave him a derisive smile. "What a touching afternoon that was for you."

"Don't be thick about this. It applies to you, too," Massimo said, his voice laced with exasperation. "You messed up, and you need to do something about that. Something more than an internet search. But this woman genuinely seems to care for you. And while I'd argue with her taste, I have no doubt about her sincerity."

Alessandro flashed to their wedding, as she'd walked toward him in the church, with flowers in her hair and a mesmerizing dress that emphasized her full belly. It was love he had felt in that church. It was love that burned inside him, and until his parents came, it hadn't turned bad. It had burned brighter all night long.

His brother put his hand on Alessandro's shoulder. "Stop punishing yourself for your teenage mistakes. Facing the past is hard and painful, but it's more than worth it. Especially when you have so much to gain."

CHAPTER TWELVE

ANN-SOPHIE HELD the baby close as he slept. She couldn't take her eyes off him. Peeking out from under the white knit cap were a few silky tufts of hair, and his eyelids were so thin they were almost translucent. His soft bronze skin, his dark brown eyes… Everything about him reminded her of Alessandro and she didn't know what to do about it.

Footsteps echoed in the hallway, and a nurse peeked in her doorway. "There's someone to see you."

Her heart took off in her chest. Had Alessandro changed his mind? Her stubborn heart thumped in her chest, hoping, despite everything that had happened. He was coming *with her belongings*, she reminded herself. And then he could leave.

"Send him in," she said, schooling her expression into something that came closer to neutral.

"I'll send *her* in," said the nurse before she disappeared out the door.

Before Ann-Sophie could register the comment, her mother walked through the door. *Her mother*, so fierce with a beauty not shaped by her features but rather, who she was. Margarita Svensson wore her years of experience etched on her face, and joy still sparkled through it. She was the polar opposite of Alessandro's mother.

"You're here," Ann-Sophie whispered.

Her mother rushed across the room and gathered Ann-Sophie and the baby in a long hug. Then she pulled back a little and gazed at the tiny new family member.

"Hello, beautiful," she whispered.

"How did you find us?"

"I came with Catarina." Her mother looked up at her. "I'm so sorry I missed the wedding. Alessandro had arranged everything for me to make it, but the storms grounded all flights and I couldn't get out."

Ann-Sophie blinked. "Alessandro did that?"

"He wanted to surprise you. So he made arrangements." Her mother gave her a searching look. "Why did you tell me it wasn't important?"

There was a hint of hurt in her mother's voice, and it twisted something inside her. "I didn't want to bother you. You were on this assignment and I wanted to ask you to come for the birth. I didn't want to ask for too much."

"*Älskling*, you have never asked for too much." Her mother's fingers brushed her cheek. "What's the baby's name?"

"He doesn't have one yet." It felt wrong to name him without Alessandro, but maybe she would have to.

"May I hold him?"

Her mother lifted the baby into her arms, and as they sat there together, the two of them in awe of this tiny new life, Ann-Sophie's heart felt a new and different kind of full, despite the sadness. Maybe, in the future, when some of this pain had eased, she could even be happy—as long as she didn't think about what she was missing. It was like her childhood, she thought with a moment of strange familiarity. As long as she hadn't focused on the loss of her father, she had been fine. And it would be the same for her and her own baby. Even though the pain of Alessandro's decision seemed unbearable right now.

"Where is Alessandro?" Her mother looked around, frowned a little. "I was under the impression that he would be here."

Ann-Sophie shook her head. "He left."

She only said those two simple words, and yet, her mother seemed to hear everything in them.

"He left you two? The day after your wedding, immediately after the birth of your child?"

"To be fair, he said that he would wait until I was strong enough. I had made him promise that he wouldn't abandon us like..."

Ann-Sophie's mother face was solemn. "Like your father."

Ann-Sophie nodded. "But I realized that I didn't want him to stick around simply because he had to. I can make it on my own. And I will. It just...hurts right now."

"Oh, *älskling...*" Her mother's arms came around her so that she was holding Ann-Sophie and the baby, and finally, Ann-Sophie let herself cry. Her tears were wiped and her head was kissed until the sadness dulled a little. When she looked up, her mother's eyes were filled with worry. But she had made it through this same situation, Ann-Sophie reminded herself. And so would she.

"Remember a long time ago, when you told me to learn the difference between need and want? I don't need him. I can do this on my own."

Ann-Sophie's mother frowned. "I'm glad that you know you can do this on your own, but that doesn't mean you shouldn't want. And there's a big difference between wanting something that is impossible and wanting something that is hard and complicated."

Ann-Sophie took a deep breath as her mother's words settled inside. This was at the center of the problem. She wanted something she believed in, something he said was impossible. And she didn't know how to convince him otherwise.

"Did he say why he was leaving?" her mother asked quietly.

"His parents are truly awful, and when they came this morning, he was angry and lashed out at them and then at me when I tried to comfort him. He feels out of control, and he…" Didn't know what to do? Didn't care enough to try? She had run through these possibilities and a dozen others. The tears began again, and she grabbed a tissue to wipe them away. "Are you ever sad that you let my father go?"

Her mother blinked, as if this was the last question she had expected. "Not at all."

"But…" Ann-Sophie sniffed. "But you gave up love for me."

Her mother's face seemed to crumple. "How could you think that?"

Ann-Sophie her head slowly. "You gave up love—"

"I chose love," said her mother said, cutting her off insistently. "*You* are the love of my life. And never for one moment have I thought I made a mistake or wondered if I should have chosen differently."

Tears welled in Ann-Sophie's eyes, and she rested her head on her mother's shoulder.

"I'm glad the baby is sleeping through this," she said with a little laugh.

Her mother stroked her hair. "You were so independent, and I didn't want to smother you, to crush your spirit. But you were at the center of my life, even when you were away."

Ann-Sophie let the balm of her mother's words wash over her. Her mother had always been a solace, even from far away, she realized. "I guess I just wish that you could have had both my father and me."

"I don't," said her mother with a sharpness that surprise her.

"What do you mean?"

Her mother looked at her for a moment, then sighed. "When you left for university, your father came back. He praised my work and told me that he had admired the way I had brought you up. Now, he wanted to work together again to see where this took them us. And I had a moment where I considered it. This was what I had hoped for when you were a baby, that he would see how wonderful having a child could be.

"But then I realized that this was actually the opposite of what I had hoped for. I had hoped that he would regret not having you in his life. Having you had changed me so much for the better, and I wanted him to experience this. But he wanted to skip over this entire part of you and me, of what our family had been, and get back to the life he wanted. And that's his right, but as he said that, I realized it never would've worked out between us. The moment we came home from an assignment and tried actual daily living together, our relationship would have fallen apart. So I told him some version of this, probably a lot less calmly and a lot less articulately, and told him to leave. And he did. I have not regretted that for one moment."

Ann-Sophie wiped a tear that had fallen and smiled, and she wondered how her heart would survive so much joy and sadness.

"Your father would have never even thought to call my mother and arrange to get her there for the wedding," said her mother quietly. "Your father was not interested in what I needed, let alone what you needed. When I spoke to Alessandro on the phone, his voice was… He was doing this for you. He wanted to make you happy. I know that this is a rough time, but I just hope he finds a way to let that happiness win."

Her mother kissed the baby's forehead and stood up, cradling her new grandchild. "Go to sleep, sweetheart. You can rest. I'll be here when you wake up. I promise."

Alessandro stood at the threshold of the room. Ann-Sophie's eyes were closed, and her mother faced her as she swayed gently back and forth. His instincts told him to back away, to leave them in peace, but he resisted. Because he could be a part of this scene if he was willing to work for it. And never in his life had he felt more willing to do anything.

So he stepped into the room, and Ann-Sophie's mother turned to him. Her movement must have startled the baby because he let out a tiny wail. Ann-Sophie's mother smiled and offered him the baby.

Alessandro was taken aback. "I don't know anything about crying babies."

Margarita laughed. "None of us do in the beginning. We all just have to figure that out the hard way."

He felt a mess of emotions bubble up, but when she handed him the baby this time, a strange calm fell over him. The mess wasn't gone, but it felt less...powerful. *Because you let yourself be here.* The baby was still wailing, so he began to hum songs he remembered, songs that Olivia had hummed to him. The baby's cries turned to whimpers and, finally, he went back to sleep. Alessandro felt a burst of pride, and he looked up, but Ann-Sophie's mother wasn't the only one watching him. Ann-Sophie was awake and watching him with guarded eyes.

"You can just put my things in the corner," she said quietly and looked away.

"I'm not here to bring you your belongings."

She turned to him, her eyes a little wider. Then she looked away again. Her mother carefully lifted the baby from Alessandro's arms.

"Why don't I spend some alone time with my grandchild," she said, and before either of them had a chance to protest, she was headed out of the room.

They were alone. Alessandro gazed at Ann-Sophie. He couldn't take his eyes off her. Her cheeks were rosy from sleep, and her mouth was parted. His mind went straight to all the ways he wanted to kiss her, to hold her, to lie with her and communicate in the best way he knew how. She looked so much like she had in his vision from the dance floor all those months ago, the one that had stopped him cold.

The thought surprised him. He was no longer scared of this vision, but that wasn't what struck him the hardest. What Alessandro found, now that the fear had left him, was *longing.* Though it had been there from that first vision, it had been too foreign to understand—because he had not let himself. Because he never believed he could have it. Now, the force of this longing hit him hard enough to send a tremor through him. He longed to see Ann-Sophie laughing on his bed. He longed to have her at the center of his life. He had longed for these things from the beginning.

Slowly, Alessandro approached the bed. Her lower lip trembled, but she tilted her chin defiantly. Alessandro fought back the frustration with himself, that he had let his parents win and she had suffered because of it. But they weren't going to win. He would make sure of that.

He sat down on the edge for bed. She had been crying, and he promised himself that he would do everything in his power to right his own wrongs, which started with an apology. "I'm so, so sorry. You told me you loved me and I walked away from that."

She swallowed, and her lower lip trembled again. "You made that choice right after our son was born."

"I didn't want to hurt either of you." He swiped a hand over his face as another wave of regret swept through him. "I thought I was doing the right thing for all of us."

"And you alone know what's best for all three of us?"

He shook his head. "I don't. Clearly."

The murmur of voices outside the room floated farther away, leaving them on their own. Together. Ann-Sophie looked so beautiful right now, from her messy hair to her flushed cheeks. Never had he been so sure of anything as he was right now. This was right. *She* was right. If she would have him.

"Why did you come back?" she whispered.

"Because it felt like I was ripping myself apart when I walked out of the room," he said quietly, and there was a starkness in his voice that he didn't try to hide.

Ann-Sophie flinched, as if hearing about his pain caused her pain. This was the last thing he wanted.

"My brother may have talked some sense into me, too," he added, trying to smile a little. "Something about my ability to care about people and how our past is not my fault. Which sounded a lot like what you were trying to tell me."

Ann-Sophie gave a wry little huff of a laugh, and Alessandro Carandini, who so rarely found himself at a loss for words, hesitated. How could he put into words how wrong he had been…and how much he wanted to make things right? He had to get this right.

"I love you, Ann-Sophie. Even when every sign pointed to it, I still resisted. That was stubborn and selfish of me, and I regret it. If you're willing to give me another chance, I will show you. And if I'm getting it wrong, I will try again." He ran a hand through his hair. "I will not walk away from this because you are what I want. I want our family so bad it hurts."

Creases had formed between her eyes, and he wondered what emotions warred inside her. The chaos of his own emotions were raining down on him: hurt, joy, sadness and…hope? Was this hope that flickered inside him, despite all the ways he had tried to bury it? But the feeling was there, burning inside him. Maybe it had been there much longer than he had realized.

It occurred to him that he was focusing on himself… again. The way he had far too often, if he was honest with himself. It was time to change that, starting now.

Ann-Sophie opened her mouth to speak. Closed it. Frowned. Then, finally, she said, "My *heart* hurts, Alessandro. And I am scared that you're going to change your mind. I love you, Alessandro, enough to let you go if you can't do this. But if you want to stay, it can't be something you check in and out of when it gets hard. You have to want more than that."

It felt as though she was seeing him. Each wound. Each fear. Each vulnerability. Could she also see the hope that flared higher, stronger, as she spoke of possibilities? He wanted it give her the same. He wanted her to know he *saw* her, so he looked into the endless blue oceans of her eyes, searching for the guarded hopes and fears she had held so closely. *I won't leave you*, he promised her silently. *I will be there for you. For us.*

"Do you want this with everything inside you?" she whispered. Her question was so achingly vulnerable, as if she was baring her soul to him.

"Ann-Sophie—" His voice broke as he spoke her name. But instead of fighting the feelings that were swirling inside him, he wrapped his arms around her and held her close. "I want this with all my heart. And I will spend the rest of our lives proving it to you."

EPILOGUE

ANN-SOPHIE TOOK one last glance at the library, then closed the door. The planning was finished. In a week, the Carandini Family Library would open to the public. She had overseen the enormous process of digitalizing the catalog that Alessandro's aunt had so carefully kept, and a small army of librarians and assistants had been hired. The training had covered everything from caring for historical material, to working with academic institutions. But most importantly, they had spent months interviewing the residents of the area to figure out what the community needed from the library, and then implementing the findings. Ann-Sophie's passion of the last year was finally coming to life.

As she made her way through the now-familiar halls of the villa, flashes from the last year came to her. But she kept going back to the days after the birth of little Emilio—named after Alessandro's grandfather—when her mother had stayed with them. Ann-Sophie had enjoyed the greatest gift she had ever received: time with the three most important people in her life…along with some much-needed support.

Alessandro and Massimo had agreed on a step to

what Ann-Sophie considered a long-overdue boundary: They changed the code on the villa's gates, ending the threat of their parents' surprise visits. It had worked. As Ann-Sophie had guessed, there was no evidence that either of his parents would change, but their harm was significantly contained. Alessandro was living proof of it. Since the day their baby was born, he had seemed to fundamentally reorient himself toward their little family.

They had also spent time in her Stockholm apartment. She loved her neighborhood and had insisted she wasn't interested in finding something larger but hadn't turned down Alessandro's suggestion for renovations to make the place easier to handle with the baby. And she definitely didn't mind the clear conversation he had had with the property-management company about a commitment to same-day fixes if, for example, the elevator broke. He was just…like that now. Sometimes, she was still stunned at the way her life had taken shape since that one fateful week in Nice.

Ann-Sophie walked outside, onto the pool deck. Catarina was floating in the water, her round belly suggesting that Emilio's new cousin would arrive shortly. Under the parasol on the far side, Alessandro bounced their little baby on his knee as he and Massimo talked. As soon as Alessandro caught sight of her, his face lit up with a smile that still felt like the sun, all heat and light. She crossed the terrace and kissed him, breathing in his warm woodsy scent, then lifted little Emilio into her arms.

"Did the final updates to the catalog go smoothly?" he asked.

She nodded. "It's all ready for next week's opening."

He stood up and tucked a stray strand of her hair behind her ear before Emilio caught it in his little hand. Then his finger drifted over her bare shoulder and onto her back, sending a shiver of heat through her.

"I'm so proud of you," he said, his voice low and private, and he kissed her again, letting his lips linger on hers. Want and need curled inside her, and she didn't try to untangle them. This feeling was a reminder of the shape the word *enough* had taken over the last year. She had always understood it as an acceptance of her missing father, but the wisdom of her mother's words all those years ago had grown to mean something quite different. *Enough* was the anchor of the deep satisfaction with what she had. *She* was enough. Their love was enough to protect them from the storms of life. This life was what she had been looking for all along.

* * * * *

If you couldn't put down Heir to Italian Altar, *then make sure to check out the previous installment in The Carandini Legacy duet,* Convenient Wife Conditions*!*

In the meantime, explore these other Harlequin stories by Rebecca Hunter!

Pure Attraction
Pure Satisfaction

Available now!